CW00797580

BODY IN THE WAY

A gripping English crime fiction thriller

DIANE M. DICKSON

THE
BOOK
FOLKS

Published by The Book Folks

London, 2024

© Diane Dickson

ISBN 978-1-80462-243-8

www.thebookfolks.com

BODY IN THE WAY is the eighth standalone title in the DI Jordan Carr mystery series.

A list of characters can be found at the back of this book.

Prologue

Lime Street station was busy in the late evening and a figure in jeans and hoody, huddled down inside his clothes, was hardly visible in the rush and dash. He hefted the travel bag in his left hand and shifted his backpack to a more comfortable position as he paced down the wide steps and out into the cold.

A cheap mobile phone was already in his hand, and he opened the mapping app. It would have been much easier to grab a taxi. It was what he would normally have done, but the only safe way now was to stick to public transport. To pay with cash, and keep his head down.

A police car screamed on Lime Street, down past the bulk of St George's Hall and off towards the river. His heart thudded in his chest and for a minute he thought he might puke, but the car disappeared into the lights of the city, and he swallowed hard and carried on walking.

He needed to get himself together, or this was all going to go wrong. Nothing new there. Everything had gone so very wrong already. This last desperate attempt to grab a chance to fix it all was a slim lifeline based on little more than hope.

Chapter 1

A blackbird sang from its perch on the corner of the roof as DI Jordan Carr walked across the car park of Copy Lane Police Station. It wasn't warm enough to leave his padded jacket in the office, but the bone-chilling cold of winter was behind them and the buds bursting on trees on the other side of the wall promised spring. He clicked the fob to unlock his car doors.

"Detective Inspector, wait on!"

He closed his eyes and sighed. It had been a long, tough day, and he wanted something to eat and a glass of wine. He was juggling several cases, and a couple of armed robberies at post offices had left staff unhurt but terrified.

It had been no surprise when Karen, DCI Josh Lewis' secretary, called Jordan's desk phone, inviting him up to the office. As he'd replaced the handset, he was aware of DS Stella May watching from the larger office. He had shrugged, and she grimaced and nodded at him. They both knew what this was going to be about.

There was no offer of coffee, although Jordan was asked to sit. Josh Lewis was in uniform; Karen had explained he had just come from another meeting and was in the office for the rest of the day. So, the hope that other pressures meant this 'chat' would be shortened was dashed.

In a traditional power play, Jordan had to wait until the detective chief inspector scribbled a couple of notes in a file, flipped it closed and turned to his desktop computer. Then, with a shuffle of his shoulders, the boss pulled a folder towards him across the desk. He nodded to himself and clasped his hands together, steepling his fingers.

"Marian Square and Park Lane, where next?" He paused and glanced up.

There was nothing for Jordan to say. He was fully aware of which offices had been raided.

"You know what I'm going to say, don't you?" Lewis said.

"Sir, it's very early days."

"Yes, but what progress has there been? What new information do you have? What is the main hypothesis? The powers that be are talking about sending this over to the serious crime squad. It's only because no shots have yet been fired that we've been able to keep it here."

"I'd be grateful if you could buy us some time. My team are doing all they can, on top of everything else they are juggling. We'll catch these people, I assure you."

DCI Lewis pushed the folder across the desk. "Look at this, Carr, the threat of violence in the second raid had one staff member needing hospital treatment for shock. I can't risk more. When firearms are involved, it's only a matter of time before there's a tragedy."

Jordan couldn't argue. They needed a breakthrough and it had to be before anything else happened.

Now, on his way out of the building, still smarting from the dressing down, he sighed again, as he turned to see a figure in uniform running across the space between himself and the door, waving a piece of paper.

"I thought I'd missed you. I tried your office…" The young officer stopped and took a couple of steadying breaths as he held out the note. "Call for you. It's personal or I would have sent it through on the radio."

Jordan took the paper and grinned. "You could have rung me."

"Yeah, I know, but I clocked you from the window. Anyway, this bloke says he's a mate of yours, but he didn't have your contact details. Obviously, I couldn't give them to him. I didn't confirm that you were here or anything, but I took his number and said I'd see what I could do. Is that okay? I thought you could give him a bell if you wanted to hook up."

"Yes, that's fine. Thanks," Jordan said.

The junior officer gave an approximation of a salute. "Have a good evening, sir."

Jordan slid into the driving seat of his VW Golf and unfolded the paper. The name scribbled above a mobile number made him grin. Peter Roper, 'Pete'. Immediately, in his mind, he was back in London, back at the gym in intense but friendly competition. They hadn't been the closest of mates, hadn't hung out at each other's homes, but they had passed time together, played in the same school cricket team and had once been in the cast of a production of Hamlet.

They had lost touch after school. Nana Gloria once told him that Pete had gone to university and was involved in the building trade in some capacity. For Jordan's grandmother, that could be anything from a bricklayer, an architect, to a multi-million-pound property owner. It was all the same to her. Now Pete had reached out and it might be fun to get back in touch.

Since the move to Liverpool, Jordan had only made a couple of close friends: Terry Denn who had been his sergeant in the early days until he'd moved on and up in his career and, of course, Detective Sergeant Stella May, whom he considered his best friend, apart from his wife, Penny. It wasn't because he was standoffish, but the job put some people off and he worked long hours in Aintree quite a way from Crosby where he lived. Penny had more people to socialise with, partly because of her work at the Citizens Advice Bureau, plus the women she met at toddler group with their son. He didn't think he was lonely, but meeting up with someone who had known him when he was a youngster was appealing.

His mates in London had busy lives, and it was rare that they could arrange a get-together. Yes, it would be good to meet up. They had followed different paths, and it had been a fair while since he'd seen Pete. He'd call him back later, after dinner, when three-year-old Harry was in bed, and Penny was studying for her Arabic language course.

Chapter 2

Jordan called Pete later that evening. His voice hadn't changed, and hearing his schoolboy nickname, 'Crackers', made Jordan grin.

At first, the conversation was stilted and halting, but as time passed and they began to reminisce, there was laughter and teasing and it was as if the many years since they shook hands on the final day at the school gates hadn't happened.

"I can't believe you're in Liverpool," Jordan said. "How did you find me, anyway?" As he asked, he imagined one of his brothers, his mum, or Nana Gloria had probably told someone who told someone else and so on. It wasn't as if there was any secret that Jordan had joined the force or that he had moved to Liverpool. But the answer surprised him.

"Well, people still talk about you, back home, and then I was in that big police station – St Anne Street, I think it is. Someone mentioned your name, and I asked if you were a big black bloke. They probably shouldn't have said anything, but I showed them the picture on my phone of us in the play and once they'd stopped laughing, one of them told me you were the DI in Copy Lane." He paused for a minute. "Shit, Jordan, I hope I haven't got anyone in trouble down there."

"Well, they've strayed a bit from the rules, but no harm done. Don't worry, I won't make a fuss. Anyway, it's just great to hear from you. How long are you in Merseyside for?"

"Not sure. It could be a permanent move. Don't judge me, but I work for Fletchers, the property developers who've recently moved into the area. They're opening an office and I'm the advance guard with the option to stay on if I like it here."

"Right. Well, we love it. The city has got a lot going for it. Tons of problems, though. I guess you can say that of anywhere, but the people are great – odd sometimes – but great and there's plenty to see. Less pressure than London, and Penny's sister lives up here too. When are we meeting up? Do you want to come here? We're in Crosby. You probably don't know where that is. I can send you the details for your sat nav. It'd be great to have you and we've got a spare room so you can have a couple of drinks or three. Oh, but maybe you're in a swish hotel and our humble little place won't be up to scratch."

"Ha, don't be stupid. Yeah, the Titanic Hotel's nice, but…"

They spent the next couple of minutes talking about developments in the family. Both Pete's parents had died. There was a momentary gap in the conversation, and Jordan heard his friend take a breath. "I was in a relationship. It's finished and when I had this chance to get away, I took it."

"Oh, sorry to hear that. Had you been together for a long time?"

"Three years just about. It wasn't working anymore, and it was a mutual decision to split."

"Right." The revelation had put a dampener on the atmosphere, and it wasn't long before the call ended with an agreement that Pete would come over the following weekend, always providing the job didn't get in the way.

Penny was giggling with her online Arabic teacher, but it was nearing the end of her lesson and Jordan poured them both a drink and took it through to the living room, excited to tell her about their visitor.

Chapter 3

Pete brought flowers for Penny, Rum for Jordan, and a wooden police car for Harry. He handed over the toy with a grimace. "Corny, yeah? Only I don't know about little kids and whatever."

Harry grabbed the car and ran to his garage, where he parked it alongside three others with similar livery. Jordan laughed and said that it wouldn't be long before the corner of the lounge looked just like work.

Conversation was stilted for a while after the initial small talk. They poured wine and sat in the living room watching Harry playing with toy cars on the carpet until Penny took him upstairs for his bath.

Jordan led Pete through to the kitchen where he was finishing the preparation for dinner and he chopped and sauteed as Pete leaned against the worktop. Slowly, they found their way back to the easy chat they had enjoyed years ago.

"So, you're definitely coming to join us up in the frozen north?" Jordan said.

"I reckon so, for a while at least. I could do with a fresh start, and I think Liverpool is big enough to keep me entertained. S'not the smoke, but I guess I'm overdue for a change."

"And it's just you for now?"

"Well, I'll have a secretary and whatever, and then some junior staff. Not quite sure what the team will look like at the moment, but this is really a preliminary visit to check out office space and accommodation, that sort of thing."

"Well, really, I was meaning more personally, to be honest, you know. God, that was clumsy. Ignore me, none of my business, and you said you'd just had a break-up… Here, can you take this bread through?" Jordan hid his embarrassment, turning back to the cooker and stirring pans.

Pete laughed.

"Ah, okay. Yes, just me. I suppose you already know about how things went after school. With relationships and whatever."

"If you mean, do I know that you're gay? Yes, of course I do."

"Right, well, there we are."

Jordan turned and grinned. He reached out and laid a hand on his friend's shoulder. "I have to be honest. I wasn't that surprised when I heard, though you never said when we were in school."

"No, I was struggling with it myself and thought it best to keep my head down. You know what it was like back then. It was rough, Jordan, and I didn't want to have to deal with what the fallout might have been if I'd come out. It didn't matter. I didn't want a relationship with anyone. I just wanted to get my exams and move on."

"Are you happy now? Now that you can be honest about who you are?"

"I was." Pete's eyes were moist, and he bent to straighten cutlery on the table. "I told you I'd been in a relationship, and it's finished. It was inevitable; I see that now, but it was hard at the time."

"Were you married, in a civil partnership? Anything like that?"

"No, we were just happy together. Me and Antony. We had a flat, a cat, the whole thing. We even met at the gym – talk about clichés. Look, is it okay if we don't talk about it? It's still raw and the reason I've made the move. One of them, anyway."

"Of course, mate. Sorry if I've overstepped."

"Nah, it's fine. Really. Now, this food smells brilliant. Are we going to eat? I can see Penny's pouring wine."

They ate in silence for a while, and then Pete asked about Jordan's career; his plans for the future. "Course, there's a lot of talk about bent coppers these days. That must be difficult," he said.

There was an awkward silence. Penny poured more wine and after a few beats Jordan said that, although the talk was hard to listen to, he had faith in his colleagues and the dishonest coppers were in the minority, as far as he knew.

"But the temptation, though. You must be offered bribes and stuff?" Pete said.

Jordan smiled, but his face was serious as he responded.

"No, it doesn't happen unless you allow it to. Now then, I think we have something special for dessert."

Chapter 4

The dinner went well. They loosened up more as the wine flowed and by the time Jordan and Pete dragged themselves to bed, the sky outside was lightening. The phone hadn't rung and the chances of a post office raid at the weekend were significantly lower, thus Jordan felt his nerves begin to unwind.

On Sunday morning, they took travel mugs of coffee with them and walked down the promenade at Crosby to see the famous sculptures of iron men variously covered by the cold, grey water. There were ships in the distance, and spread across the flat, damp sand were joggers, walkers, and dogs. Jordan and Pete sat on a low concrete wall together and the awkwardness of the previous night returned, but neither of them knew why.

Jordan cleared his throat and gulped back the last of his coffee. "So, after breakfast, do you fancy the Pier Head, the ferries? It's corny, I know, but it seems to be where we take visitors and Harry loves it."

"D'ya know, Jordan, I've had a really great evening, and the dinner was brilliant, but I reckon I might get off. Not straight away. You promised me breakfast if I remember rightly." Pete turned and smiled. He patted Jordan on the shoulder. "It's great catching up, but I've a big day tomorrow looking at more premises and tonight I have reports to write. Let's take a rain check, and next time I'll invite you and lovely Penny out for dinner. If you're okay with leaving Harry. Next week, maybe, or lunch, Sunday, if that works better. The hotel's got a couple of restaurants. And just to be clear, I'm sorry about some of the stuff I said last night. You know that garbage about bribes and what have you. It was the booze talking, mate."

"If you're sure. We have a good babysitter and we both enjoy a night out. Dates are more special when you have to think about them. Listen, mate, if there's anything I can do, any help at all, just give me a bell. My personal mobile is best. As for the other stuff, you're not the only one who thinks we're all on the take. We just have to prove it's not true, don't we?"

It was early afternoon by the time Pete left for the hotel with a promise to call in the week.

* * *

"He's great, isn't he?" Jordan said. He'd wrapped his arms around Penny and nuzzled her neck. She could feel him smiling and turned to kiss him. It was good to see him happy and relaxed for once.

They were clearing away the dishes after the brunch, and Penny paused on her way to the kitchen.

"He seems nice. I don't remember you mentioning him much. Gloria showed me the pictures of you in the play once. I'm sure she thought you were destined for the West End."

"He wasn't one of my closest mates, but we always got on." He stepped back to get a better look at her face.

"You haven't got those pictures, have you?" Penny said.

"Nah. They're down in London."

"It's interesting that he's got them on his phone."

"What do you mean, interesting?" Jordan said. "You've got that look on your face."

"What look?"

"The one where you're not sure about something, but you don't want to say."

"No, no, I haven't. I just thought it was odd for him to have them on his phone. I mean, they are old, and as you say, you weren't best friends. You haven't even kept in touch. He's gone to the trouble of digitizing them."

"Well, his mum and dad died. Perhaps he just transferred some when he was sorting out their stuff."

"Yes, that's very possible. Why didn't he ask Gloria or your mum for your number, if he knew he was coming to Merseyside?"

"I dunno. What is this?"

"Nothing. Nothing really. I just wondered why he got it from St Anne's Street. Did he say?"

"Yes, he was in there and he heard my name mentioned."

"Right. So, why was he in the station in town? How long has he been up here?"

"I don't know. Jeez, I didn't ask him."

"Sorry, this is a daft conversation. It's great that you've hooked up and, yes, he seems nice. Hey, why does he call you Crackers?"

"Oh that, it's just one of those daft things. You know the biscuits, the ones for cheese, well… they have the same name as me, don't they? I used to eat them a lot when Nana Gloria had us on diets after my dad died. You know her and Mum went over the top for a while wanting us all slimmed down and fit. They were scared we were all going to have heart attacks. Probably right, I reckon, but it was a bit of a drag for a while, and I used to nibble those bloody biscuits to stave off the hunger. They were cheap."

"Oh, it's not because you were a bit of a nutcase, then?"

"No, it was not. Seriously though, you did like him, didn't you? I mean, you don't mind meeting up again?"

"No, it's fine. Really."

Chapter 5

All was calm when Jordan arrived at Copy Lane on Monday morning. He had time to sit with Stella for a coffee and a catch-up. He told her about his weekend and the old mate turning up. She told him about her trip to a London theatre with her upstairs neighbour.

"It was fantastic," she said. "I didn't think I'd like a musical, but once I got into it, I loved it. Going with Keith and his new boyfriend was great as well, they've been to loads. That's me. I'm an expert now. Never been before, loved it, probably never go again, but just ask if you want to know anything." She laughed. "I've only been to London twice before. 'That London', Granda calls it, and he was convinced we were going to get mugged."

"If I'd known, I could have suggested some good places to eat," Jordan said.

"Oh, we just had some chips and beer in a pub. Honest to God, it was really brill."

Stella would have raved on if the call hadn't come in with a report of another robbery at another post office. They grabbed their coats from the backs of their chairs and stormed out of the office. They were joined by DC John Grice on the way to the car park.

"What do you know, John?" Jordan asked.

"Altway Post Office. Sounds like the same people. Three of them, two in the shop and one stayed in the car. This time, they used a blue Mercedes A-Class. They seem to like Mercs. DC Webster is checking the stolen vehicle reports. If it's like last time, it'll have been nicked. They wore ski masks and goggles, same as before."

"Send Kath a message and tell her to scan the recent reports to see who's missing a blue Merc. Start local and then widen the search and tell her to get DC Purcell on the PNC to help. They'll be fine. Kath and Vi both know what's required. They've been at it long enough. Are there any injuries?"

"No shots fired, but the punter that made the three-nines call asked for an ambulance. The alerts are still coming in," John said.

"Okay, we'll take Stella's car so I can read the reports. You follow us, John, in case we have an injury and need someone at the hospital. Have you got the directions, Stel?"

"I have. I know that one on Altway, anyway. It's inside a convenience store; well, it's a small supermarket. Shouldn't take more than five minutes as long as the bloody school run doesn't get in the way."

By the time they arrived, patrol cars had blocked the access road. a personnel carrier was parked in the main carriageway with a uniformed officer trying to keep the traffic moving. Crime-scene tape was fastened from bollards and lamp posts. An ambulance had drawn up outside the mini-market. The rear doors were open and there was no sign of the paramedics. Jordan showed his ID to the constable with the clipboard and ducked under the tape, with John and Stella close behind.

Inside the shop, a small group of people were huddled together near the counter. A uniformed officer stood alongside. They were all focused on the activity near the post office counter, where two paramedics crouched over the prone body. A blond woman was on her back. One of her furry slipper boots had fallen off and been kicked aside. There was blood smeared across the tiled floor and sullying the side of her pink fluffy onesie.

She was obviously unconscious and, as they watched, the paramedics fixed a cervical collar around her neck and carefully slid her onto a backboard.

"Is she all right? Is my mam all right? Oh God, is she dead? She's not dead, is she?"

Jordan turned to see a policewoman wrap an arm around the shoulders of a teenaged girl who had dissolved into a flood of tears.

"We only came for some ciggies and a frozen pizza." She sniffed and wiped her hands over her face. "We didn't even want the post office. She asked me to come, and I wouldn't and it's all my fault that she's here."

One of the EMTs looked up at Jordan and grimaced. "We'll take her to Fazakerley Emergency. She's not so good," he murmured, with a quick glance at the distressed girl. "Will one of you blokes come? I reckon we need to take the girl as well, but she shouldn't be left on her own. She's only a kid. This is tough for her."

Jordan glanced at John, who nodded. "Do you want an escort?" Jordan asked the paramedic.

"That'd be ace, mate. It's a bugger getting through the commuters at this time of the morning."

"DI Grice will arrange that for you, then."

They waited until the woman had been wheeled out and the sobbing teenager escorted to the ambulance, and then Jordan turned to the group of onlookers.

"Okay," he said, "we'll need to speak to all of you. Is there somewhere we can go and maybe someone can make everyone a hot drink?"

A tall, thin woman stepped forward. "You can use my office. My name's Lilian Goudy, call me Lil. I'm the manager. Christ, this is awful. Look at this." She held out her hand, which was shaking uncontrollably. "I'll get someone to put the kettle on. We all need something hot and sweet to drink. I don't believe this. What the hell is happening to the bloody world?" She turned to the group of bystanders. "Julia, put the 'Closed' sign up on the door. They'll have to go without their pensions this morning. If there's anyone desperate, tell them to go up the Old Roan." Then, more quietly, she addressed an older woman in an overall who was sobbing as she wiped at one of the shelves with a yellow duster. "Mrs Finch, Amy, could you put the kettle on, love?"

Jordan nodded at the officer, who took the duster from the cleaner's hands and escorted her into the rear space.

"See that?" Stella said quietly.

"What's that?" Jordan said.

"Well, wiping the shelves. That's just like my mam. When anything happens that she can't control, she brings out the hoover and the Pledge."

"I guess she was just working on autopilot. Mind you, someone needs to have a word with that plod. She should have stopped her cleaning. It's too late now anyway, and it's at the other side of the shop. We'll mention it to the SOCO team, so they're aware."

They followed Lilian into the back area of the shop and the overcrowded office.

Once they were seated on assorted plastic and wooden folding chairs, Jordan opened his notebook.

"We'll need any footage from your CCTV. I noticed the cameras. Can you arrange that?"

"Of course," Lilian said, "I'll have to clear it with my bosses but there won't be a problem. Don't know how it'll help with them all covered with those bloody hats, though."

"I thought pensions were paid through the bank these days," Jordan said.

Lilian nodded. "Mostly they are, but there are just a few who haven't got bank accounts or, you know, they like to hold the money in their hands. Seems more real to them."

"So, how much money was there?"

"Not much. I'd need to check. The shop takings are banked every night, so it was really just the float; we were waiting on the cash delivery for the post office counter. It should have been here earlier, but they were held up in traffic. There's been an accident down town. Chaos and upset everywhere today." Lilian sniffed loudly as tears ran down her cheeks. She swiped them aside with the ends of her fingers and squared her shoulders.

"So, they were disappointed?" Jordan said.

"Yeah, I tried to tell them, but they were just yelling and waving that gun around. We were all scared stiff. Jean, that poor woman on the floor, started shouting at them. She was so mad, she told them they were no marks and she was going to call the bizzies – sorry, that's just what she said. She told them they should get jobs." Lilian made a noise, part sob, part laugh. "She doesn't put up with anything, doesn't Jean. Anyway, he hit her. The bigger one. He just turned round and swung at her with the gun. She'll be all right, won't she? I mean, she only came in for her ciggies."

"She's in good hands," Stella said. "Listen, I need to have a word with the others out there. Can I use your staff room?"

"Yeah, of course you can. Anything, just anything. The evil buggers – where do they get guns from, anyway? I just don't know what this country's coming to."

At last, Lillian lost the struggle for control. She began to sob.

Jordan looked at Stella and raised his eyebrows. It was going to be a long morning.

Chapter 6

DCI Lewis paced back and forth in front of his desk. "This is exactly what I was worried about, Carr. These people are running riot in my area, and we are doing nothing to stop them." He paused to glare at Jordan.

"I don't think that's fair, sir, sorry. We have been working hard but there's very little to go on and these raids have come out of the blue. No reports on HOLMES 2, nothing on the PNC. We are literally starting from nothing. I can assure you we are working as hard as we can on it. We have more information since this morning's event – a better description of two of the suspects. We've already found where the car was stolen from, and we're reviewing CCTV of the area. That's over in Woolton and I'm sending someone to interview the owner later; see if they'd spotted anyone hanging around, that sort of thing."

"Hmm." Lewis nodded. "What about the woman who was injured?"

"John is still at the hospital. She's very poorly. Hasn't regained consciousness yet, and they are concerned for her."

"Keep me informed. I will probably have to give a media statement later and I must show how concerned we are about harm to the public. I'll have a word with St Anne Street and see if you can carry on for now, but you know as well as I do that the clock is ticking." He flipped the cover on the file closed and stretched a hand towards his in-tray.

Jordan stood and, mumbling 'thank you, sir', he left.

When he returned to the incident room, Jordan's small team were all busy either with their heads down in front of their computers, or on the phones. He paused at his office door to let them know that there would be a meeting in an hour, and he needed an update on all open cases before they reviewed the interviews from the post office robbery.

"I know you're all working flat out," he said, "but this must take priority. We now have a member of the public seriously injured. So, if possible, clear your decks and I'll try to get us some more help."

Stella had forwarded notes to everyone about the interviews that she had conducted with the shop staff. Jordan hadn't had the chance to collate his notes, but he would let them all listen to the recordings, which would suffice for the time being. John had messaged from the hospital that Jean Court had deteriorated, and the medical staff had called in the remainder of her family, a son, and a widowed mother, who were now in the Critical Care Unit awaiting developments. Jordan sent a more junior officer to wait at Fazakerley and messaged John to return to Copy Lane immediately he was relieved.

The first task was to go around the room and find out which of the several cases they were handling could be shelved or put on the back burner for the time being. A missing teenager last seen wearing her school uniform and boarding a train to London was to be passed to the missing-persons unit and a spate of carjackings in the supermarket car park in Aintree which needed hours of CCTV footage to be monitored, could wait until more staff were available. Jordan hated doing it and knew that, for the people involved, delay caused added upset, but with staff and funds in such short supply, there was no choice.

It was no surprise to anyone that the interviews had elicited differing accounts of what had happened. Different things stood out and fear and trauma confused memories. Two of the staff had been in the back rooms and only run into the shop in reaction to the noise. One other woman, Julia Bull, had hidden behind the counter, and the cleaner, Amy Finch, who had been in the shop for the whole of the raid, had been incoherent, sobbing and muttering without making sense.

"I think someone should see her later at her home," Stella said. "Maybe in her own surroundings she'll be more help. All she kept saying was that she'd only worked there a couple of weeks as if that made a difference."

Jordan turned to the whiteboard and listed the descriptions they had been given.

Two perpetrators inside the mini-market – probably both males. Young or perhaps not so young. Tall or average. Everyone agreed they thought at least one of them was white. The mask that he wore was not the balaclava type and had left a little skin on his brow exposed. They had both worn hoodies pulled up over their heads, jeans, and boots. The other was described as skinny and that was repeated enough times, so Jordan underlined the comment. "If they all mentioned that, then maybe he is abnormally thin." It wasn't much, and it was confused, but there were enough similarities with the other two robberies to convince them it was the same people.

Their biggest hope was pinned on Amy Finch, who had been there the longest and apparently froze to the spot watching the situation unfold. Lilian Goudy had been behind the post office counter and by the time she had moved into the main shop, nearer to the men, Jean Court was screaming at them, and the ensuing attack had taken her attention. The robbers had turned and run off empty-handed when the customer had fallen to the floor in a spatter of blood. Lilian had dashed to the door in time to see them dive into the rear of the car, but didn't have the wherewithal or opportunity to note the licence number. This admission had produced another flood of tears and Jordan left the manageress sobbing into the arms of Julie, who seemed to be a sort of second in command.

The bobbies who were there first had spoken to people outside. Their accounts were confused, but one of them had managed to get a picture of the car as it sped away. The image had already been sent on to the IT department and all fingers were crossed that it had in fact caught the registration.

Next door, the confectioners had been busy but by the time the customers in there heard the screaming from inside the post office and realised what was going on, the car was off and up the road.

It wasn't a lot, but DC Kath Webster and DC Violet Purcell were working hard to track the blue Mercedes that had been seen speeding away shortly before the call had come in to the emergency operator.

"The last couple of times, the car was found pretty quickly – burned out on spare ground – so probably that's what you should watch for. I've had an alert sent out to everyone. The car is out there somewhere," Jordan said.

John arrived back just in time to be sent out to visit Amy Finch at her house.

It was late afternoon and Jordan sent Penny a message to let her know he would probably be late. He was stalking around the office, waiting for something to show. He had written his report and viewed the CCTV from outside the shop over and over, but he left the tracing to Vi and Kath, who always came up trumps with this work. He wished he had gone with John to interview the cleaner, but it was too late, and he couldn't turn up now and undermine the detective constable.

There was a buzz of excitement when a message came through from the digital imaging lab with confirmation of a registration plate.

Stella was busy winding up a couple of her outstanding cases and preparing to submit documents to the CPS to persuade them to prosecute a rape case.

It was frustrating, but Jordan felt he couldn't go home and leave the others working. In order to assemble his thoughts into some sort of order, he scribbled notes on a pad.

Through the open doorway, he saw Kath turn from her desk to high-five Vi, who sat next to her. Taking a moment to give them a chance to calm down, he walked over to where the two women were chattering together over the screen.

Chapter 7

Kath's eyes were wide with excitement, and she stood to give Jordan a chance to see her screen.

"ANPR has picked them up at Fazakerley Hospital. I don't know where they've been until now, but they haven't been there more than a few minutes. We can try to trace them back later. For now, control has been informed, and an alert has gone out to all cars in the area. Everyone is on the way. Do we need to alert the firearms unit?"

The situation was dangerous, but Jordan held back from calling in the armed response team. The thought of guns in a hospital was terrifying. He should let the DCI know. A chain of command would need to be sorted. Still, he held back. Radio reports were coming from the officers in cars who had by now closed off access to the A506, Lower Lane, and Longmore Lane. Officers on the spot were searching the hospital grounds. It was a huge site. In the multistorey car park, two cars screeched round and round the ramps and between the aisles of parked vehicles. Others trawled up and down between the buildings. There were patients and visitors everywhere at this time of the day. And out there, a man with a gun. In the incident room, there was a tense silence. Jordan saw one of the civilian clerks had her eyes closed. She crossed herself, her lips moving in silent prayer.

"Boss, armed response!?" Stella hissed.

But he held up his hand. "Wait, let's just wait," he said. "But get on to the hospital security, tell them what's happening."

She spun away to stomp to her desk, teeth clenched, and her hands bunched into fists. And then they heard it. The vehicle was abandoned in the multistorey, slewed across the road. There was nobody inside.

The relief was very brief when followed by the realisation that this might mean the armed men had accessed the hospital buildings, leaving Jordan no choice. There must be a firearms incident declared. They had to protect the patients and staff; it was the priority. He lifted the phone.

"Weapon secured, repeat, weapon secured." The woman's voice filled the room. "We've closed off access. No sign of anyone on foot. Officers are searching stairwells and other levels. We could do with as much backup as possible here."

There was a communal sigh. Stella flopped onto her chair as she made the call to the hospital. Vi and Kath hugged each other. Elation was cut short. There was still work to do. The gun was no longer a threat, but three heartless yobs were at large in a place filled with vulnerable members of the public.

Jordan grabbed his coat. "Kath," he called across the room from near the door. "Call the DCI, bring him up to date. Tell him DS May and I have gone to the hospital, and we need as much backup as he can arrange. Great work, by the way. Vi, call the security at the hospital again. Tell them we're going to have as many people as possible to help to search. The men may no longer be carrying firearms as far as we know, but they should still be considered very dangerous. They should lock down; the multistorey is out of bounds to everyone for the time being. I know it's going to cause mayhem, but there's nothing else for it."

As they ran down the corridor, John was passing through the door from the car park.

"Come with us, John," Jordan said. "I'll fill you in on the way. Have you got a stab vest in your car?"

John nodded.

"Grab it."

Stella stopped to pull her own protective gear from the boot of her car and threw it onto the backseat of the Golf beside Jordan's. In the car on the way to Fazakerley, they listened to the Airwave reports from officers on the ground. They had been joined swiftly by the hospital's own security team and a search was underway. It was impossible to do it without attracting attention, and pictures of the force's presence and speculation about terrorism and bomb threats were already circulating on social media.

DCI Lewis had been declared gold command, and he sounded livid when he called through to Jordan's phone on the hands-free. "What the hell do you think you're doing, Carr?"

"I made a judgement call in a rapidly developing situation, sir."

"And look at the mess we are in now. Armed men rampaging through a hospital. The internet swamped with panic and speculation, and half the city's troops engaged in this debacle."

"I'm on my way there now, sir. The gun has been secured." What else could he say?

"Right, you're silver command on this for the time being until we see how much backup you need. Keep me informed. Get on with it. As soon as you have the chance, let me know the situation."

They were already at the hospital. They didn't take time to weave through the vehicles parked on the access roads.

Leaping from the car, they ran, holding up their warrant cards as they went.

The head of security for the hospital met them at the main entrance. He was tall, just past middle age and beginning to spread around his waist. His face was red, and he was panting. Sweat stood out on his forehead, and he wiped it away with the back of his hand.

"Jesus, what the hell is going on? Are you in charge?" He pointed at John, who shook his head and opened his mouth to speak. He was interrupted. "Which of you is in charge?"

Jordan showed him his ID and introduced Stella and John. "For the moment, I am silver command on this. How much do you know, Mr…"

"Scott, Mike Scott," the man said. "Right. One of your blokes came up to my office, going on about armed men in the car park and needing access to the CCTV. Next thing there are bloody uniforms everywhere, roads blocked off and total mayhem. This is unacceptable."

"Well, it seems to me that the officer you spoke to was on the ball and did just what was necessary." Jordan didn't have time to be complained at. He stepped into the building as he dragged on his stab vest. "Okay, where is the CCTV suite? We need to see as much of the site as possible. The officers in uniform are going to search carefully and if the men we're looking for are in your hospital, we'll find them. They are no longer armed with a gun, as far as we know."

"As far as you know. Bloody hell, mate, what's that mean?"

Jordan took a breath and turned. He was a little taller than the security chief. He stepped in close and leaned forward. "It means we don't think they are armed with a gun any longer. That doesn't mean they don't have other weapons and we must be prepared for that. Now, we haven't got time to stand here discussing semantics. My sergeant" – he pointed to Stella – "will go with you to the monitoring room and myself and DC Grice are going to the car park. Please, make sure your team are aware of the danger and let's just deal with this and discuss it once we make sure your hospital is safe. Yes?"

With a grunt, Mike Scott turned and stormed away up the corridor with Stella running to catch up.

* * *

In the car park, there was an officer guarding the abandoned Mercedes. Police swarmed between cars on the other floors and peered into electric cupboards, lifts, and stairwells.

Jordan bent to look inside the car where the gun lay on the rear seat. "Nobody touches this car until the SOCO team gets here."

With that, he spun on his heels and headed for the exit. "No point in us dashing about like blue-arsed flies, John. Let's find Stel and get a better overall picture."

"Are you going to declare a major incident, boss?"

"Probably we'll have to. I'd hoped they'd be collared quickly, but there's no choice now. It's a manhunt. I'll call the DCI and we'll get things sorted."

Before he had the chance to dial, Stella's name came onto the screen. "Boss, the bike storage, three men together, hoodies, jeans, and boots. They didn't come through the hospital, just from the car park."

Jordan called to one of the hospital security team, who was dodging between parked cars. "You, take us to the bike storage. Now."

Chapter 8

Jordan, John, and the hospital security guard charged from the car park, between the buildings, and around the front of the hospital. Outside on the small concourse, groups of visitors, staff, and patients – some of whom were attached to drip stands and slouching along in slippers and dressing gowns – were milling about in confusion while police officers tried to keep control.

Jordan waved a hand towards the door. "Get everyone inside. It's all under control."

Stella was keeping up a running commentary on an Airwave set so that everyone could hear, but it was disheartening.

"Jesus, they're quick," she said. "The bikes look like mountain bikes. Didn't have time to pick up on the colours, they went straight to them, they knew they were there. They've gone off down past the ambulance station, heading for Brookfield Drive. Get somebody after them. If they get into the rough over there, it'll be hell to catch them."

Sirens screaming, two patrol cars shot past the front entrance.

Jordan stood, hands on hips, panting slightly after the run. He shook his head. "Bugger."

They listened to the search and the alert going out to all units and they knew that with three males on bikes, out in the rough among the trees, they would need the devil's own luck to catch them.

"Get on to Hawarden Heliport," Jordan told John. "Let's put the helicopter up."

Although he'd been made silver command partly due to the DCI's sloping shoulders, it did at least mean he could make this decision. There would be questions and recriminations if the men got away but for now, he would pull out all the stops.

"Call Kath," Jordan continued, "we need to have something out in the media as quickly as we can and keep as many mobile units as possible searching. If they've split up, if they've changed their tops, or anything like that, we're on a hiding to nothing."

He turned and watched as the crowd shuffled back inside the building, police officers jogging away to rejoin their cars and take part in the widening search. Mike Scott stood in the doorway, ushering people inside, nodding and smiling, shrugging his shoulders at the comments as people passed.

He jerked his chin towards Jordan. "So, now what?" he said.

"We need to review all your footage from the cameras. It's pretty clear they knew those bikes were there. I mean, what are the chances? Three mountain bikes handy just where they needed them. So, when were they left here?"

"We can look for that and I can ask my staff. But quite a few people come on bikes."

"Let's have a look anyway, okay? The bikes didn't park themselves in the shelter."

"Your circus, mate." With that, the security chief turned and walked back through the door, leaving Jordan and John to follow him.

The technician went quickly back through the hours while the bikes had been in the storage shed. Eventually, very early in the morning, three people rode up, passing close by the main doors. Their hoods were up, effectively hiding their faces. They were dressed in jeans and rain jackets. The bicycles were parked and secured and then, heads down, the three entered the hospital.

"That's them," Stella said. "Sure as."

"Yes, I reckon so. Can we follow them on the cameras inside?" Jordan said.

The technician nodded and, as he scrolled and clicked, switching from screen to screen, they watched the three men separate and make their way through the maze of corridors until they left through different doors and were lost in the grounds of the facility.

"Can you download everything that has them on and let my colleagues have copies?" Jordan said. "We'll get it to our IT technicians. I don't think we'll see their faces, but there are other things to watch for, gait and demeanour, the type of trainers and tops, all of that. It's interesting that they seem to know their way around the place."

"Well, they only need to visit a few times. The signage is good," Mike Scott said. "I hope you're not insinuating that they're staff?"

"I'm not insinuating anything. We have to look at all the angles. Stella, I'm going up to the HDU. I've got my phone on vibrate. Call me if there is anything significant."

Jordan left them watching the screen and listening to the reports as the hunt for the three cyclists continued more and more unenthusiastically and it became clear they had escaped.

The helicopter had been delayed at a traffic accident, but now it could be heard overhead. Jordan stood for a minute to watch it sweeping over the landscape. Round and round but never locking on and following. It was too late, they were gone.

* * *

In the critical care unit, it was a world away; hushed, calm and quiet, with only the sounds of equipment and the murmur of staff and visitors. The nurses were twitchy because they had been told to lock the doors, but when Jordan showed them his warrant card and told them the drama was over, they allowed him in. The officer who had been left to stand watch was nowhere to be seen. Jordan made a mental note to give him a bollocking until he was told that Jean Court had lost her fight for life just over an hour ago. While the thugs responsible had been careering around the grounds, she had quietly slipped away and now her family sat holding her cooling hands in a curtained-off cubicle, trying to process the sudden change in their lives after what had begun as an ordinary Monday with the need for cigarettes.

Chapter 9

The day was giving way to a rapidly deepening dusk. Lights flicked on along the roadsides and in the shops and offices. Three cyclists sped along the road on a quiet industrial estate. They switched and swapped position in line and one of them, the skinny one, flicked the front of his bike upwards, pedalling forwards on the rear wheel alone. The other two let go of the handlebars and waved their arms in the air, whooping and yelling as they swerved back and forth along the narrow road.

Skidding between tall metal gates into a junkyard they jumped from the bikes, running behind the decrepit buildings to hide them under a tatty tarpaulin.

One of them dragged a key from his pocket and unlocked the Judas door of a storage unit. Once inside, they ran to the rear, snatched open a discoloured old refrigerator, and grabbed a six-pack of lager.

"Jesus, Stick, what a buzz, what a fuckin' buzz, man," said the keyholder, wiping sweat from his forehead and sucking at the frothing can. Beer dribbled down the front of his sweatshirt and he rubbed at it briefly.

"I know, I know, Benno. That was boss. The filth didn't stand a chance. Fuckin' no marks. Brain dead trolls – oh, man!"

The third flicked at the seat on the scabby old couch before slumping onto the grubby cushions. He sat with his head back and his eyes closed, the unopened can loosely held in one hand.

"Hey, Daz, you okay?" the one called Stick asked. He was jigging from foot to foot, twitching his shoulders and nodding his head to some sort of internal rhythm.

"Okay, you ginger moron, am I okay, did you say? Christ, what are you like? Both of you. Where are you at? You do realise, don't you? We've lost the gun. Benno left it on the back seat. The soddin' gun." He swept his fingers through the dark, wavy hair, dragging it back from his brow, and shook his head. "You were supposed to be in charge of it."

There was a brief silence. "Well, yeah, I know, it's a real bummer. I know. But there was no way I was going to carry it on the bike, and we had to shift pretty bloody quick... What? Did you want me to get nicked?" Benno said.

"We should have used the van, like before," Daz said.

"I didn't know Frank was going to an auction, did I?" Benno whined. "We could have put it off. We could have done it another day when we had the van. It was all crap, not like before. There was bizzies everywhere. I didn't like your idea with the bikes, not from the start. It was naff. Who ever heard of robbers on bikes? That's cringe."

"Fuck off, man. It was a good idea. We got away, didn't we? You were supposed to put the gun in your backpack," Daz said.

"I was spooked, Daz, it'd gone wrong. I was shittin' myself."

"But the gun, man," Daz said.

A darker mood descended now, and the other two slid onto the sagging seat and slurped their drinks.

"They won't be able to trace it, though, so no worries. We always wore gloves and wiped it with a hankie and all that. We were careful. Okay, we don't have it anymore but to be honest after that old biddy it's maybe just as well," Stick said.

"How d'ya mean, like?" Benno said.

"Well, I know she was asking for it and that, and Daz lost it with her. But we weren't supposed to hurt anybody."

"Oh, she'll be fine. Stupid old cow. I only gave her a bit of a belt. She was just puttin' it on for attention," Daz said.

"Yeah, I know, but there'll be blood, won't there?" Stick said.

"Blood?" Benno screwed up his nose. "Oh, gross. Was there a lot of blood? I mean, you just said he bashed her with it. Was there a lot of blood?"

"Yeah, it splattered on the wall and then she fell on the floor," Stick said.

"Shit, man. Are you sure she's okay?"

"I said, didn't I?" Daz snapped. "There might be blood on the gun though, that's true."

"Well, there will be, and you can't get rid of it. It gets in the bits and you can't get it out," Stick said.

"So what?" Benno muttered, throwing the empty can into an old bin and popping open another.

"Well, they'd know it was the one. If they ever did catch us. Not that they could, I know that. I'm not saying that, just, if they did, like, they'd know it was the gun that hit the old cow," Stick said. "All I'm saying is that now that it's got, like, blood on it, we're best rid of it."

"Yeah, yeah," Benno turned to Daz. "He's right, Daz, better off rid, innit."

Daz opened his eyes and glared at the two of them. "So, what now? Where are we going to get another one?"

"Another one?" Benno said.

"Yes, shit for brains. Where are we going to get another one? Won't be as easy next time, will it?"

"Well, why do we need another one?"

"Oh, Christ," Daz said. "If we aren't tooled up, how are we going to do the post offices? We was going to do betting shops next. How are we going to do them without a shooter? What, you just going to wag your dick at them? Yeah, that'll scare them."

"I dunno, Daz," Stick said. "I mean, it's been a blast and that, 'course it has, but I dunno about doing more. They could have caught us today."

"Caught us. Did you see them? Were you there? They didn't have a bloody clue. Of course they couldn't catch us. Anyway, we agreed, we get enough together so we can go to London, and we haven't got enough for that yet."

"Have we not?" Benno said.

"No, course we haven't, not unless you want to sleep in a stinking hostel. That's not the plan, I'm not doing that. I want enough so I can rent a place, enjoy myself. I want a stake in the game."

"Yeah, but how much have we got? Have you checked it?" Benno said.

"Of course I've fucking checked it. There's about five, thou."

"Well, that's loads," Benno said.

"Don't be a dick. It's nothin'. You haven't got a clue. Do you know how much it costs to get a place down there? We're not goin' on holiday, least ways I'm not. Once I get away from here, I'm not comin' back."

Benno dropped his gaze and picked at the top of the can. "Yeah, I know that was the plan, like. I know you want to get away, away from that bloke your mam's with and his bastard kid, but going for good, I dunno. I mean, I like it here and my mam and dad'd be dead upset. I like working with Frank, he gets me. What would we do?"

"Oh, grow up." Daz waggled his head and put on a high, whiny voice. "'*My mam and dad'd be upset*'. All you're bothered about is where your chips are gonna come from and who's going to pay for your trabs. I'm off. I'll see you tomorrow. Keep your heads down and don't be stupid, if you can help it."

Daz uncurled from the sagging seat and threw the half-empty can towards the bin where it landed on the concrete and spun, spraying the contents across the floor. He flicked a hand through his hair and straightened his jacket; then, without a backward glance, he stalked from the unit, and they heard him pulling his bike out from under the tarp.

"Bloody hell, look at that. Uncle Frank'll be pissed if he sees that." Benno leaned towards a small side table and tore off a length of paper towel, which he used to mop up the spilled beer.

"Do you want to go to London, Stick? I mean, yeah, I want to go, like, but do you want to go for good? You know, never come back? Was that the plan?"

"I dunno, mate. I hadn't thought. I mean, I know Daz wanted to, but I didn't think we'd ever do it, really. Look, he's just pissed because we lost the shooter. He'll be all right tomorrow and we can talk about it then. It's been ace, but I need to go. I'll see you tomorrow. I'm goin' into college to finish a project and I'm gonna be late. They said it's good enough to go in a competition."

"Yeah, what competition?" Benno burst open a bag of crisps and offered one to Stick, who shook his head.

"Well, an art competition, of course. What did you think?" Stick pulled on his fingerless, Lycra gloves and jogged to the door. "Tomorrow, in the affie." With that, he left.

As Benno locked up the storage unit and turned to retrieve his bike, tears pooled in his eyes and mixed with the fine drizzle that had started while they'd been inside. He rode off between the closed-up buildings but the sound of the helicopter overhead turned his stomach and he was forced to stop and throw up the beer he'd just drunk. They'd hurt someone. They'd put a woman in hospital. Everything had gone wrong. This wasn't the way it was supposed to have been.

Chapter 10

The search had slowed down and turned into a 'be on the lookout for'. The helicopter had gone back to base. It was rare that it went home without a result, but they had tried until the fuel was running low and there was nowhere logically left to search. After all, how far could a cyclist flee? There were hours and hours of CCTV recording to watch. It had to be run slowly, the contents noted separately, and Aintree was a busy hospital. The surrounding area was filled with residential, commercial, and industrial sites.

The case had been elevated to homicide; they had a code-name for it – 'Operation Oak Apple' – and everything was different.

Now, there were clear criteria and specific actions to follow. No one wanted a case thrown out because of stupid errors and deviation from the rules. The images of the robbers lifted from the hospital CCTV were online, in the paper and on television, along with a warning that the men should be considered dangerous. There was little more that could be done right now, and Jordan walked through the incident room, updated the whiteboard and poured himself a mug of only slightly stewed coffee.

"Why does everyone call it Fazakerley when it's Aintree?" Jordan asked as he stopped beside Kath's desk to watch her start on the mammoth task with the videos.

"Habit," Kath said. "I guess it takes a long time before people are ready to register the changes. Mind, it's not like it was – they knocked the old one down. All three of Vi's kids were born there, and my daughter. It was either that or the Women's – one of those dead old places, like a workhouse or something. Good care, I think, but even the older Fazakerley Maternity was more modern in its day."

"Well, good luck with this. We've got a couple of extra constables joining us tomorrow. Don't know how long for, but it'll take some of the strain."

"I'm on it, boss. You know I enjoy this. We'll do our best and we'll trace them back and check where they were in the few hours before they turned up at the hospital. We'll see where the buggers went afterwards, with a bit of luck. Mind, three lads on bikes, not going to be easy."

"That's interesting."

"What's that?"

"You said 'three lads'. What makes you call them lads?"

"Okay, well, first we know they're male. Then the way we saw them move, they look like younger blokes and their clothes are more like kids' clothes, aren't they? I mean, in the earlier video, when they dropped the bikes off, the thin one's wearing skinny jeans and they've all got designer tops."

"Yes, I reckon you're right. Thing is, though, they were armed. Where the hell did young lads get a bloody gun? Have we received the report back from the lab yet? Do we know what sort of gun it is, where it might have come from?"

"Not yet, but they're backed up down there, aren't they?"

"Hmm, I'll see if I can give them a bit of a push. Where's Vi, by the way?"

"Just gone to the bog. She'll be back in a mo."

"Oh, erm. Okay. Listen, Kath, don't stay too late. It's been a long day for all of us and we need to have a break so we can get back to it tomorrow. We are going to be putting in long shifts until this is over. I'm just going to write up my reports, will be about an hour. John and Stella are back over at Amy Finch's. They took some stills of the suspects. At least she might be able to confirm who it was that hit Jean Court. It's also an excuse to check on her; make sure she's okay."

Jordan wrote up his report and sorted tasks for the next day. The hardest, he kept for himself. Someone needed to interview Jean's daughter, and that was not going to be easy. They had been allocated a family liaison officer who reported that they were all at home now, shocked and grieving.

By the time he arrived at his house in Crosby, Jordan had missed Harry's bedtime but tiptoed into the bedroom to give his son a kiss. The child was over three now and getting too big for the cot. They were going to have to buy him a bed. He felt a jolt of sadness at the thought. His baby was growing up quickly. For a minute, he was swept by panic and fear. How did you make sure they grew up well? Was it possible to avoid them falling in with the wrong crowd?

Penny came to stand behind him and they watched the little boy sleeping. She wrapped her arms around Jordan's waist and kissed the back of his neck.

"Come on, love. You're exhausted. I've poured us a drink and dinner's almost ready. We can watch *Game of Thrones* afterwards, take your mind off the violence and… Oh wait!" She laughed again, and took his hand to lead him out of the nursery.

Chapter 11

Jordan was in the office early. At half past six, it was well before the morning roll call or his briefing with the team. He expected to be on his own. As he pushed open the door, the smell of fresh coffee made his mouth water.

Stella was at her computer. There were papers spread around her and a grease-stained bag stood on the desk corner.

"Boss." She grinned as she glanced up at him. "Didn't think I'd beat you in, but nah nah ne nah nahh."

He laughed as he poured his drink.

"I've got us pastries," Stella said. "A bit like old times, eh?"

"Yeah. Shame it's under these circumstances."

"Well, is it though? When else would we be mad enough to be in when it's still dark outside and anyone with any nous is still tucked under the duvets?"

"True. I'd like to say we should do it more often, but really, I don't think so."

They allowed a few minutes to enjoy the warm croissants and coffee, and then Jordan screwed up the paper bag and tossed it into the bin under the desk. "I'm going to shoot an email to the Ballistics Intelligence Service. They've had the gun since yesterday. They're going to laugh at me for asking for progress, I know, but I need to keep us in their minds. I know I shouldn't say this, but if they'd used the gun, we would have been better off in a way."

"God no, boss. You definitely shouldn't be saying that."

"I know, but perhaps a gun that hasn't been used won't get the attention that a used one would."

"Maybe not, but we don't know that it hasn't been used, do we? Not until we find out just where our suspects got it. So, if it has, they'll match it up pretty quickly, I would have thought."

"Yes, that's a point. In the meantime, could you see what tasks the computer's thrown up and allocate them ready for the briefing? Thanks for the breakfast."

The team was keen, and everyone was in by seven. There would be house-to-house enquiries in the residential and commercial properties around the hospital and they would go back to the area near the post office. DCI Lewis had managed to second several uniformed officers who were not thrilled to be going out in the cold drizzle that had come with the dawn. Most of them, however, were keen to be part of a major case.

Jordan had already pencilled himself in to interview Jean Court's family and for Stella to interview the owner of the blue Mercedes. He would have sent Kath, who was more junior, because it was low priority, but she was better getting on with the job that she excelled at, so she and Vi were to be left in front of their screens.

* * *

The fence in front of Jean Court's house was broken and in need of paint. There was a short, paved path which was full of weeds and wanted brushing. The paint on the window ledges was flaking. The UPVC front door was streaked with dirt. Generally, the place was downtrodden and decaying. They had checked with the Land Registry to find she had owned the house.

The previous evening, John searched social media and read several mentions of Jean on Facebook, mainly on the daughter's page. There were pictures of her at the local junior school where she had worked as a dinner lady. In another post, she was smiling happily at a birthday party in the confectioner's shop on Altway. A bout of shingles had seen her claiming sickness benefit and laid off from work. She had been married, but according to what was posted, her husband was long gone and living in Scotland with a nurse. Their daughter, Milly, kept in touch, but Jean never appeared in the pictures of the other family. Jordan wondered about her son, a twenty-year-old living at the same address. It didn't seem that he was pulling his weight with the maintenance of the house.

The curtains were closed on all the windows and Jordan checked his watch. Half past ten. He rang the bell.

A dishevelled Milly Court opened the door. She peered out at him through red-rimmed eyes. Behind her, in the hall, Jordan could see the family liaison officer who raised a hand in greeting.

"I'm sorry to bother you, Milly," he said. "Can I come in?"

She didn't speak but stepped aside to let him pass and followed him down the hallway, her bare feet shushing on the carpet.

"I hope I didn't get you out of bed," Jordan said.

"I haven't been to bed," Milly said. "I can't close my eyes. Every time I do, I see that again. In the shop, that bloke bashing my mam."

She began to sob, and the FLO stepped forward and led her to the settee.

"I'll put the kettle on, shall I?" she said.

"Thanks, Aisling. It is Aisling, isn't it?" Jordan said.

"Yes, that's right, boss."

"It's gloomy in here, Milly. Do you want me to pull back the curtains?" Jordan said.

"No, you can't do that. Nan says we have to keep them shut until the funeral. When will that be? I can't believe it – my mam's funeral. I don't know what to do."

"It's horrible for you, I know. We're working hard to find these people and that's why I'm here. Maybe there's something you've remembered now that will help us. Sometimes things come back hours and days after a horrible thing happens, and they might be really important."

Milly sniffed. "Won't bring her back though, will it? Even if you catch them, it won't make any difference to us. She'll still be gone."

Jordan had heard this many times and there was no answer. All he could do was move on.

"Is your nan here with you?"

"No, there's just that Aisling woman, but she didn't stay overnight and there was supposed to be another copper, but she never came. Nan had to go home to look after her cats. She's got two."

"Okay. Well, is there anything you've thought of that you didn't mention yesterday?"

The girl made a show of thinking deeply, but then shook her head. "No, they came in just after we got there, like I told you. They were pointing that gun at the woman behind the counter and shouting. There was so much shouting. My mam just walked up to them and told them they were no-marks and to bugger off. They wouldn't listen. She got more and more mad. She couldn't half get mad. Well, then he just sort of turned around and swung that gun at her and she went down. It hit her. I heard it hit her. Then they ran."

"Did they speak to each other? Did they use names?"

She shook her head slowly from side to side. "No, I think I was screaming by then and that cleaner had run to the door after them. Then we heard the car, and they was gone. I didn't do nothing. I didn't. It was like I was frozen. My mam wasn't scared of them – she wasn't – and now look where it got her."

Aisling had brought the tea, and while she fiddled about with sugar and spoons, Jordan looked around. The room was clean. There were family pictures on the mantelpiece and a bag of knitting wool with needles poking out, next to the fire.

"What about your brother, Steve, isn't it?"

The girl turned away. She pulled at the edge of a cushion squashed into the corner of the settee. "He's out."

"At work?" Jordan asked.

"No, he's out with his mates. They've been out all night." When she looked back, her eyes were flooded with yet more tears.

"Why has he been out all night? That's not very nice for you, being on your own in the middle of all this."

"They're looking for those blokes. Our Steve says he's going to find them and when he does, they'll pay for what they've done."

Jordan sighed and blew out his cheeks. "That's not a good idea, Milly. You know that, don't you? Can you call him? Does he have his mobile with him?"

"It won't do no good. I can't tell him what to do."

"Does Steve know who they are? If he does, he would be best telling us, letting us deal with it. Trying to find them himself can only end badly. He must leave it to us. Give me Steve's number. I'll talk to him. As for the rest of it, I'll move things along and let you know as soon as possible about your mum and when you might be able to arrange a funeral."

"Can't we have her now, straight away? Nan wants her brought home so we can have a vigil and that. I don't know about it, but we'll do what she wants. She's old-fashioned, and she was a kid in Ireland. It's what they do."

Jordan didn't have the heart to tell her that there was going to be a post-mortem examination the next morning. The idea of her mother being cut open in the morgue might just be a step too far. More importantly, he needed to speak to the son and avoid more tragedy for this family.

Back in the car, Jordan called the station. He alerted them to the added complication the conversation about Steve Court had thrown up, and asked everyone involved in the house-to-house to be made aware of it. There were images of him on the social media pages, and Vi was tasked with sending those out to the troops on the ground. They couldn't arrest him because he had done nothing wrong, but if he was found, they would ask him to attend Copy Lane to answer questions.

Next, Jordan called Stella and arranged to meet her at Amy Finch's house. He wanted to check on her and find out whether their witness was any more able to answer questions.

Chapter 12

Stella was parked outside Amy Finch's house before Jordan arrived. She had spent the time filing the report of her interview with George Wilson, the owner of the blue Mercedes. The car had been parked in front of his large, detached house and he'd returned from a business trip to find nothing but an empty space on the flagstones where it usually sat.

He had reported it and been given a crime number; he grumpily accepted that, as he didn't have a tracker fitted, it was all that was going to happen. Now, though, when he saw the image Stella showed him and confirmed that it was his missing car, he had told her he didn't want it back. When Stella had queried that, he just told her that '*he couldn't bear to drive it after it had been in the hands of such low lifes*'.

His other car, an Alfa Romeo, was locked in his garage, protected by CCTV cameras and an alarm. When Stella asked about the security, hoping for CCTV images, he shrugged his shoulders.

"Horse gone, stable door bolted," he had said. "All that was fitted yesterday. I know better now than to leave my keys near the door, though. The security bloke reckons they'd use a computer to download the codes to get access and start it. Of course, I've got no proof, but I don't see how else they could have taken it. Anyway, I've learned some lessons. I've got a Faraday box now, ready for when my new one arrives. The sods won't best me again. As far as I'm concerned, it's gone. I want nothing to do with it."

Stella had told him they would need his fingerprints for elimination purposes and he'd agreed, with a large sigh, to attend the local station before the end of the day, '*if he could fit it in*'. There had been a few further questions, but he hadn't seen anyone hanging about and, anyway, he'd been away for several days and couldn't say exactly when the car had been taken. The house was an imposing, detached property with bay windows and a large garden. It was surrounded by a yew hedge that effectively hid it from the road. The fancy wrought-iron gates had only a simple latch, and Stella suggested something more substantial would be a good idea.

"This is a good area," Wilson said. "I suppose that means we should expect this sort of thing. But it's a Neighbourhood Watch area and next door has a dog."

He wasn't really interested in what Stella had to say, but she noted it might be worthwhile canvassing the area when they could spare the bods.

Jordan joined her to interview Amy Finch. The woman appeared to have aged in the short time since they had seen her on the morning of the robbery. Her hair was lank and greasy. She was dressed in a pair of trousers with pilling around the knees, and her beige jumper had seen better days. She peered at them through the half-open door.

"We're really sorry to bother you, Mrs Finch," Stella said.

"Go away. Leave me alone. I don't want to talk to none of you. Just bugger off, that's all." She began to push the door closed and Jordan laid his hand on the wood.

"Are you all right, ma'am? Do you need a doctor?"

"Why would I need a doctor? I'm not sick, am I? I just want to be left alone. Go on, get off my path."

Jordan assumed she was afraid and tried to reassure her. "Do you want me to arrange for the patrol car to pass by regularly?" He held out his business card. "Take this. It has my mobile number on. You can call me any time if you feel scared. Or call Stella."

"No, I don't want a bloody patrol car coming past. I want you to leave me alone."

They had no choice. She had told them to leave and so they must. With a final reassurance that she could call them any time, they left her to slam the door, then heard the locks clicking into place and the rattle of a security chain.

"Poor woman, she's really been shaken up," Stella said.

"Yes, one of the invisible victims, I suppose. Nothing we can do if she won't talk to us, though. There were only three of them there the whole time. Her, Milly, and Jean Court. Jean can't help us and I don't think we're going to get much more from Milly."

The post-mortem exam was pencilled in for later. Jean Court had died because she was struck by a violent robber. The finer points didn't matter until they found someone to put in front of a judge. But Jordan still felt duty bound to attend.

Chapter 13

Benno was pushed into a corner of the stained couch. There were sweat marks in his armpits, and he wiped away perspiration beading on his forehead with the back of his hand. He picked up his mobile and called Stick again. It went straight to voicemail. He left another message.

> *Call me, you shit. Call me. I'm bricking it here. Come to the yard. For fuck's sake, answer me.*

He dialled Daz's number and crossed his fingers but there was no answer. He didn't bother with a message. He couldn't see the point.

He threw the handset to the other end of the seat, where it bounced against the arm. He went back to scrolling on his tablet. Tears pooled in the corners of his eyes, and he wiped snot from below his nose with the back of a finger.

The big doors swung open, juddering as they caught on the dirty floor. His uncle Frank stopped to finish a cigarette and grind out the end on the puddled gravel.

"Oi, you. Lard Arse, put that sodding tablet thing away and get your bum in gear. I need you to go up to Park Lane and pick up a cooker from an old woman there. She said she'd have it left in the front garden. For God's sake, lad, smarten up. Look at the state of you. Your belly's on show with that naff T-shirt. When did you last have a haircut? You're my representative and you look dead grotty. This might be a scrap yard but we're not bloody scumbags. Come on, move yourself."

"I'm busy, Uncle Frank. I'm, like, doing research."

"Research my balls, get off that couch."

"I can't get a cooker on my own."

"No, well, call one of them useless mates. The ginger, skinny one or that poncy one that thinks he's God's gift. I'll bung them a twenty."

"I can't. Stick's at college and I've been trying to reach Daz and he's not answering."

"Well, get one of them and take yourself up to Park Lane before I come back. I'm going down the betting shop."

"I'm not supposed to drive, Frank. I've only got a provisional."

"Aye, says you. It's never bothered you before. You weren't so fussed when you wanted to go gadding about here and there, were you?"

"No, but I don't want to get picked up by the bizzies, do I?"

"You'll be fine. Just drive carefully. It'll be okay."

Dragging on an anorak, Frank turned and stomped to the door. "The address is on that paper, on the table. Don't leave it too late. I told her I'd do it today."

Benno went back to the tablet on his knee. It was addictive. The local BBC, ITV, SKY, the *Echo* website. There were posts on X and Instagram. It was everywhere. It was everyone's dream to go viral but not for this. Not for some dead granny. He had looked at the police website but when he thought they might be able to monitor who was browsing, he clicked off it and deleted the link. It was everywhere. That bloody old woman was dead. They'd killed her. Daz had killed her. Okay, he'd been outside in the car, but he knew how this would go. He would be part of it. What would they say? An accessory. He'd been scrolling through legal advice sites. He couldn't ask on Quora because that could be traced back. It was pretty clear, though. If one of them was caught, they were all in it, up to their necks. The cereal he'd had for his breakfast rolled in his stomach and he pushed the computer aside to run to the toilet where he vomited it up, as well as the two cans of coke he'd had afterwards.

Back in the big room, he picked up the phone. There was a message from Stick.

> *Been in the art room all morning. I told u. What's to do? I'll c u this affie.*

Stick didn't know. How could he not know? He dialled his friend's number. It was answered after three rings. Before Stick spoke, Benno yelled into the handset. "She's dead. Jesus, Stick. She's only bloody dead. What are we going to do?"

"Who's dead, moron? You're not making any sense and stop yelling at me."

"That woman, the woman from the post office. The woman Daz belted. She's only dead. Shit, man. What are we going to do?"

Chapter 14

Hours and hours of viewing CCTV footage had netted very little. They had seen the car speeding away from Altway, but after that, it was lost to them. It must have been hidden until it was picked up later in the afternoon, heading for the hospital.

Jordan went into the incident room where everyone was tired and jaded. "Okay, I think that's enough. Everyone is bog-eyed with it and that's how we miss things. It's near enough to end of shift. Call it a day and we'll start again tomorrow."

"Boss, tomorrow I want to go back to the other two robberies. We weren't looking for bikes back then," Kath said.

"Yep. That's a good idea. We'll just keep going until we find them."

It was frustrating so when Stella suggested a drink in the hotel down the road from the police station, Jordan jumped at the chance. They would end up talking about the case; there was no question about that, but maybe away from the computers and the whiteboard with the image of Jean Court and the gun that had ended her life, their minds would be clearer.

"What did they do?" Stella said. "There were a few hours between the robbery and them turning up at the hospital. They waited until the heat was off before they showed themselves. If it wasn't for Kath and her picking up the ANPR report, we would have missed them."

"Aye," John said. "If we had, I suppose they would have parked the car there in the hospital and just ridden away on their bikes. It was the sirens and what have you that spooked them. So they didn't have time to park up properly."

"Okay then, what did they do between turning up at the hospital and the robbery in the morning?" Jordan said. "They don't show on any of the traffic cameras until Kath spotted them. It was smart because while we were running about like idiots, they were just hidden away, waiting for things to calm down. With the other two robberies, the cars turned up soon afterwards – burned out on waste ground."

"Is Kath checking the hospital bike storage for the other two dates?" Stella said.

"Yep, that's part of what she's going to do tomorrow. But it doesn't really work because the other cars were found in completely different locations. At the hospital, there are hundreds of people coming in all day and well into the late evening, so it'll be very difficult to find them, even though we know the time. That's why it's so clever. Maybe we should see if we can get an expert in gait to have a look at pedestrians. We've used somebody at the university before."

"I agree, it was clever. They're pretty switched on, I reckon. I wonder though what made them change their routine. It's not by a lot, but it is a change," John said.

"Yes," Jordan said. "Could be just to keep us guessing."

Stella opened her tablet and put in a search on Google Earth.

The racecourse was a vast open space in the middle of what was otherwise a heavily built-up area. They would have to canvas hundreds of houses and it just wasn't viable. Jordan stared at the map on the screen.

"So, where would you hide? Middle of the day, busy area?" Jordan said.

"I suppose you could just go to work. Get yourself an alibi and then meet up again later."

Stella took a gulp of her gin and tonic and then nodded. "Okay, so you probably wouldn't be in an office. Not in the hospital, not dressed like that."

"They could have changed, of course," John said. Then he shook his head. "But why change back if they were trying to avoid being spotted? It would need to be somewhere with a car park. What else is there around there? It's your stomping ground, Stel."

"There's everything, isn't there? Shops, schools, industrial units. Okay, we can discount shops, probably."

"Industrial units are a possibility, and we can probably cover them as long as we're allowed to keep the extra bods. Add that to the tasks for tomorrow," Jordan said.

"I'm done now, boss. I'm absolutely knackered." Stella turned to take her coat from the back of her chair. "We could all do with a break. I'll be in early tomorrow. Shall I get some breakfast?"

"Oh right, count me in if there's going to be bacon," John said.

It was almost dark, and there was a fine, icy drizzle. Lights were coming on early and there were very few people about. As he drove through the quiet streets of Crosby, Jordan tried to focus on the cosy home and the warm welcome waiting for him but all he could see was the tear-stained face of Milly Court in the gloomy house with no company except for the family liaison officer.

As if he'd conjured up the call, his phone rang as he turned into the drive. It was Aisling, the FLO. Steve Court had turned up in a foul mood. His ranging around the streets with mates had, not surprisingly, turned up nothing and had simply left him exhausted, angry, and sad.

"He's told me to leave, boss," Aisling said. "Said he doesn't want me there. I'm worried for Milly, but there's nothing I can do. I've told him to leave it to us and that he's only storing up trouble, but I don't think he'll listen."

"Okay, don't worry. Did you pick up anything of any use?" Jordan said.

"Don't think so, no. They are destroyed, all of them. The son was horrible, but I still felt sorry for him. I worry he might not give up, but let's face it, unless he has an idea who it was, he's as much in the dark as we are."

"You're right, Aisling. Right now, things are pretty grim. We don't want another robbery and we don't want anyone else hurt, so we need to keep at this. Listen, can you keep in touch with Milly? Let me know how she gets on. I'll call in as soon as I know when the body is going to be released. It'll give me a chance to speak to her again, and have a word with her brother."

Chapter 15

Benno and Stick sat side by side on the couch, staring at the tablet screen, scrolling through the news reports and the appeals for help. Benno chewed on a breakfast bar, but Stick simply gnawed at his fingernails, which bled where he had bitten them to the quick.

"Try him again," Stick said. He picked up Benno's phone and thrust it into his hand. "Try him."

"I've tried him a gazillion times," Benno said. "I've tried him till his message box is full. All I can do is send him another text, and he hasn't answered any of them. We've got to go round there."

"I'm not going round there. I'm getting rid of the bike. It's going in the canal. Soon as it's properly dark, that's going."

"There's no need. We'll break 'em up and stick 'em with Frank's scrap. That way, we don't need to take them out in the road," Benno said.

"Yeah, ace. We'll do that. Let's do that now."

The door juddered open, and Frank was silhouetted against the faint light of the darkening sky. "What the hell? Why has my van not been moved? Why is there no clapped-out cooker in my yard? I thought I made myself clear. I told that old bird I'd collect it today. This is my word you've broken, and I'll not have it. Get off your fat backside and get up to Park Lane or you're out of a job, nephew or not. You as well, Skinny, you owe me. You come here, drinking my ale, eating my crisps and riding round in that van just when it suits you. Then I ask you to do one small thing and you can't be arsed, either of you. Get out now. Take the address and get yourselves up to Netherton."

"We can't, Frank. We can't go out." As he spoke, Benno felt the sharp sting of a kick from his friend.

"What the hell do you mean? *You can't?*" Frank said. "Of course you bloody can. Unless you've broken both your legs, you can get out now."

"I've got a bad gut," Benno said. "Don't want to go away from the bog. I need to stay here."

"Oh aye, is that why you're sitting there stuffing your face with oatie bars? You think I was born yesterday? Get on, both of you. Out now or we're finished, and I'll tell your mam just why."

* * *

The van clattered into life. Benno swiped tears away from his face and stalled the engine as he tried to reverse across the yard.

"Shit, man," Stick said, "this is, like, yikes. I'm not kidding. We must be mad. We'll get nicked, sure as."

"Shut the fuck up, man, I mean it, just button it. Let's just go and get this pigging cooker. Then we're goin' round Daz's. We're out anyway. Look, it's probably okay. It's the bikes they're all talking about. The bikes and the Merc. Nobody mentioned the van. They don't know about it from before. We're all right. Honest to God, we're okay."

The brave words didn't do anything to hide the tremor in his hand or the crunch when he messed up the gear changes.

The wipers on the old van battled against worsening rain and when they reached the house in Park Lane, the dilapidated cooker stood in the middle of a sodden lawn. It was covered with a wool blanket, wet through and stinking. As they heaved the gas stove across the grass, the door opened and an old woman yelled at them to 'mind her daffies' and complained about the late hour to be collecting junk. They turned their faces away from her and crouched over the load, hiding under the dripping hoods of their soaking tops.

Lights were shining at Daz's house in Aintree. The curtains in the downstairs rooms were drawn across, but the upstairs windows were fully lit. Stick picked up a piece of gravel from the path and tossed it at Daz's window. After a couple of minutes, they tried again, but there was no response.

"We'll have to knock," Benno said.

"Aw, man, what if that bloke answers, the one screwing his mam? He's horrible, is he? And he doesn't like me since I peed in his flowerpot that time." He raised his head and cupped hands around his mouth. "Daz. Daz."

The front door flew open and, to Stick's relief, Daz's mother stood in the porch, her arms folded across her chest. "What the hell are you doing? Benno, is that you?"

"Yes, Mrs Burdon. We was looking for Daz– erm, Daniel."

"He's not here, is he? I thought he was with you. I haven't seen him since this morning. He said he was going to college. Yeah, and I believed that as much as I believe I'm gonna win the EuroMillions. But he hasn't come back. Try his phone. He'll be up to no good somewhere. Now bugger off and leave decent people in peace. I see you, Stick, you was told not to come round here anymore."

"Sorry, sorry, Mrs Burdon. If he comes back, will you ask him to ring us?" Benno said.

They turned away and slouched back to the van. "Daz wasn't at the college, was he?" Benno said.

Stick shook his head. "Course not, he hasn't been coming for ages, not properly."

With no idea what to do next, they drove back to the scrapyard, unloaded the cooker, and spent an hour dismantling their bikes. Benno's was no great loss, and he flung it onto the pile of scrap without much thought, but Stick had to swallow back sadness as he threw his pride and joy onto the heap. He removed the silver charm that he'd hung on the handlebars the day he'd brought the bike from the shop, and pushed it into his pocket.

"I might tell my mam it was nicked," he said.

"You can't do that, you dork. What if she makes you go to the cop shop and report it?"

"Shit. So, that's the end of that, it… it's just gone."

"We've got five thousand pounds between us. We can buy new bikes. You can tell your mam you repainted it. She'll believe you, tell her it was a college project."

"Yeah, I can do that. Ace. I reckon we should tell Daz we want some of the money," Stick said.

"Yeah. Stick…" Benno paused. "I don't want to do it no more. I know it was a buzz and that, but now that woman's dead, I really don't want to do it. I'm devvoed. They showed pictures of her with her daughter. This has gone too far."

"Yeah. Let's tell him. We'll find him tomorrow and we'll tell him. Even if he gets mad, he can't force us. He was the one who hit that woman. We can threaten to go to the rozzers with it. Anyway, we haven't got that gun no more and I don't think even Daz knows how to get another one."

"I wish I'd never found it. I think this is all my fault," Benno muttered. "Never mind, we'll share the money, and then he can go away if he wants. I don't want to live in

London." He smiled for the first time that day. "I'm going down the chippy. You coming?"

Chapter 16

Jordan had his phone on vibrate as an alarm, so he didn't disturb his wife. There was no need. When it woke him at half past five, the other side of the bed was empty, and he smelled the scent of coffee and toast drifting up from the kitchen. Penny had laid the table and when he walked in, she turned the grill on over a pan of bacon.

"Oh, this is nice," Jordan said. "You needn't have got up."

"I know, but we hardly saw each other yesterday and I can use an hour to study for my course before Harry wakes up. By the way, I thought we might go and buy him a bed this weekend if you can take a couple of hours."

"Yeah, of course I can. I'll make time. Where do you fancy going?"

"Don't mind, but I'd like to get him a proper one, you know, not self-assembly. It feels important and when I think of all the years he'll spend in it, I think I'd like something a bit special."

"Yeah. I'll ask around, find out where to go. John Lewis is the only place I can think of. There must be others."

"That'd be fine, actually, and they're sure to deliver. So that's a date, then?"

"It is."

She put two plates on the table with bacon and egg toasties and they sat in silence as the sky brightened and the birds in the garden emitted a cacophony of song.

"We should go down to the shore one day. Watch the daybreak over the water. Maybe there's still snow on the Welsh hills," Jordan said.

"Hmm, that sounds nice. Another date as soon as you can."

"Oh, talking of that, I reckon I'll give Pete a call and tell him this weekend is looking dodgy and put it off for a while. I'd rather do that than let him down at the last minute."

"Oh yes, listen," Penny said, "Nana Gloria called yesterday. No problems. She wanted your recipe for that sauce you put on the ribs."

"Wow, Nana, asking for my recipe, I can die happy," Jordan said.

"Yeah right. You know she'll change it. Anyway, I asked her about that Peter."

"Oh, oh, '*that Peter*'. You don't like him, do you?"

"Don't know him well enough to make a judgement. But I thought he said he'd found you from a comment in St Anne Street?"

"Yes. That's what he said."

"Only Nana Gloria said he'd been to see her a couple of weeks ago. Said he'd seen you were in Liverpool, but he wanted to know just where."

"Oh. Well, maybe I misunderstood. Or maybe she told him, and he forgot."

"Well, I'm just saying. That's what she told me."

"Look, if you really don't like him, I'll just let it slide. I'll call off this weekend and then keep my distance."

"No, no, it's fine. It's nice for you to have someone from London to talk to. I don't mind at all. By the way, you've got egg on your shirt."

"Oh balls. Right, well, I'll go and change, then I'm off. You have a good day. I'll try not to be too late, but the way things are..." He shrugged.

"Yes, I know."

She stood and kissed him on the forehead as she cleared away the plates, and by the time he came back downstairs, he could hear her in the dining room practicing her Arabic pronunciation.

* * *

Stella and John had beaten him to the office, and he'd forgotten about the breakfast arrangement, but he could always find room for another bacon roll. They scanned the overnight reports and sorted the tasks that would have to be allocated. Most of it was house-to-house canvassing to catch the people they still hadn't spoken to, or yet more CCTV for everyone.

"Kath made a good point yesterday," Stella said. "About the bikes at the sites where the other cars were burned out. I don't want to step on her toes, but I can get on with that right away. I'll confer when she comes in, of course."

"Right. I'm going to the post-mortem this morning. In the meantime, let's make a start at the places around the hospital – the industrial units, mainly. I don't suppose anyone has seen a report about the gun yet?"

"No, nothing. Like you said yesterday, boss, it wasn't fired, even though it caused the death of that poor woman. The requests for DNA and blood tests went in before we even passed it on to the BIA, but they won't be back this week, I don't reckon."

* * *

James Jasper, the medical examiner, was already into his day by the time Jordan arrived at the mortuary near the School of Tropical Medicine in the city centre. The pathologist was changing his protective overalls as his previous subject was wheeled away. He dragged off the paper hat, which covered his thick mane of grey hair.

"Jordan, just in time. I was about to start on your lady. Poor thing. I've got a couple of students with me today. No problem for you?"

It was posed as a question, but Jordan knew better than to refuse. It never took much to irritate Jasper. The mortuary assistant winked at Jordan as she passed him a hat and gloves and then turned away to help a colleague prepare Jean Court for the indignity they were about to visit on her remains. There were three students, two male and one female. They all looked nervous, but whether that was the anticipation of the examination or fear of getting on the wrong side of the medical examiner, it was hard to say. Jordan knew he'd probably be okay. This was far from his first post-mortem, but one of the boys looked decidedly green and his fingers shook as he pulled the paper hat over his gelled hair.

Chapter 17

Jordan felt sorry for the student who'd dashed out of the room with his hand covering his mouth and his face decidedly grey, but it was just one of those things. Jordan had coped at his first few examinations, even though he was convinced that he had been singled out to attend the ones that would be the most gruesome. Sheer determination to prove he could do it had seen him through.

Jasper looked up and tutted, shook his head and then continued to remove the top of Jean Court's skull with his electric saw.

The brain was removed and sliced and there was a degree of tutting; Jasper called the students nearer to point out what he had found. The medical jargon was lost on

Jordan, but he knew he would be given a more understandable account in the fullness of time and, with luck, over a cup of coffee in Jasper's office.

After it was over and they walked into the corridor, they saw the missing student sitting on a bench, bent forward with his head between his knees, and a plastic cup of water on the seat beside him. Jordan hesitated for a moment. He could tell the lad it would get better, maybe try to make him feel less embarrassed. However, before he had the chance to speak, Jasper's voice boomed out. "Get back in the room and help to clean up."

It seemed harsh, but of course, it was Jasper's way of getting the young man back into the room and forcing him to witness some of the mess and gore.

The coffee was good, as always, and there was even a Hobnob biscuit on the saucer. Jasper made much of settling himself behind the desk and pushing papers around. Jordan had seen the performance before and knew it was the precursor to a bombshell of sorts. He braced himself.

"Right, well," Jasper began, "there was significant damage to the bones of the skull, and we already know how that was inflicted. The measurements and location will be in my report. However, the cause of death was not the blow to the head." He paused and looked across the desk. There was a glint of amusement in his eyes, or maybe smugness.

"Not the cause of death?"

"No. Mrs Court succumbed to a CVA. A cerebrovascular accident or, to put it even more simply, the lady died from what you would probably call a stroke. Haemorrhagic."

"The blow didn't kill her?" Jordan said. He was struggling now to collect his thoughts. "That's bleeding in the brain, isn't it? So, the assault was to blame?"

"It wouldn't have helped, of course, but having looked at her blood vessels and general health, and reading the reports from the hospital, I have to say that she was living on borrowed time. A long-term smoker, significantly overweight with what was most probably a poor diet, this was going to happen at some point. Her blood vessels were absolutely clogged up with fat. I don't know whether this will make her family feel any better, but despite all evidence to the contrary, she wasn't murdered."

"But without the blow to her head, would she have lived?" Jordan knew that when Jasper made his conclusions known, there was no moving him, but he still tried.

"I think you know better, Detective Inspector, than to ask me what is bordering on a stupid question. Of course I can't answer that. I am not God or his opposite number; though I would appreciate you not letting that information go beyond these four walls. One has a reputation to maintain. But, to answer your question to the best of my ability, I would have thought that were she fitter generally, in better overall health, shall we say, Mrs Court would more than likely have survived. She would have suffered a vicious headache for a while but would have gone home to her family in due course."

"Manslaughter," Jordan murmured.

Jasper shrugged. "Not my decision to make, nor yours, I would suggest." The medical examiner slapped the top of his desk with his large palms and pushed his chair backwards. "Time you left. I have more subjects waiting for me and a student I want to force back onto the horse as soon as possible before he allows himself to imagine that he is unable to observe without puking. He shows promise. I'm not letting such a small thing as a craniotome get in the way of his future."

Chapter 18

The news about the cause of death caused confusion and debate. Jordan stood near the whiteboard and waited for the room to quieten.

"Okay, this was unexpected, but it changes nothing. It doesn't matter that the victim may have died soon from natural causes. She may not have. She may well have gone on for a long time. Even if she hadn't, she would have had more quality time with her family. She would not have spent her last hours unconscious in the hospital as a direct result of that thug hitting her. So, as far as I am concerned, we continue to search for them with the same vigour as before. There isn't only the assault, there are the other robberies and the danger of more. We need to find these people and bring them to justice. Quickly."

"Are you going to tell the family?" Stella asked.

Jordan looked at the pictures of Jean Court and imagined Milly's tear-stained face. "I haven't decided. The coroner will notify them, anyway. I don't want them to think that we are not taking this seriously."

"It may calm the son down," John said. "If we say that his mam wasn't murdered."

"I doubt that", Jordan said. "I don't think it will change his mind at all. It's still going to feel as though she was killed at the post office. So, for the moment we just carry on working as we were. This is a change, but not for us."

Jordan turned to Stella. "Stella, what about the bikes? Was there any sign of them near where the other cars were abandoned?"

"Trouble is, boss, something like that draws a crowd. Loads of kids and many of them are on bikes, scooters, skateboards, everything. We are having to single out each bike to see if the person with it fits the description of our suspects. I'm working with Kath on it, but it's slow going."

"All we can do is keep at it. Everyone else, I reckon we should be out around the hospital. At least we know for certain that they were there."

Nobody groaned, but Jordan knew by the set of their shoulders and the drag of their feet that the team was becoming downhearted. The original buzz had gone. They needed a breakthrough. Soon.

Jordan poured a mug of coffee and went into his office. He didn't usually spend much time in there. It was small, and he didn't enjoy feeling cut off from the team, but he wanted some quiet, and time to straighten out his thoughts. The thieves were fit, that much was clear. They had been away on those bikes and into the woods before the patrol cars could catch them. So, they surely must be young; Kath could well be right describing them as lads. But how did lads have access to a firearm, and why would they choose violence and robbery? Did they realise the danger they were in? Did they not worry about the repercussions, years in jail, or worse, that they could be mowed down by armed officers? There had already been one tragedy, there mustn't be any more.

Lads, but old enough to drive, maybe. Unless you were picked up for a traffic offence, Jordan knew that there were drivers on the roads with no licence, no insurance, banned for one thing or another. But maybe they just needed to look old enough.

He went back out to the incident room. He addressed everyone who was still there.

"Let's have a really close look at the local schools and colleges, particularly those with sixth forms. Check the car parks for the Mercedes during the day on Monday. Also, the bike sheds."

There was a ripple of laughter at the old term and the implications. "Bags I go with Stella," John said. "What about it, Sarge, you and me behind the sheds for a quick fag?"

"Yeah, and what's your Gil going to say about that?"

"I won't tell her if you won't."

"She'll report you to the prefects, and you'll be in detention," Vi said. The gentle ribbing lightened the mood, at least.

"So, you're thinking schoolkids, boss?" John said. "That's a chilling thought. Mind, nothing would surprise me these days. Trouble is, they see all these computer games and I think they forget that it's not like that in real life. The cartoon people."

"I think you mean the avatars, John," Stella said.

"Whatever they are, they get up after they've been killed, and that's the wrong message to send to youngsters."

"I'm not thinking twelve-year-olds," Jordan said. "They must be old enough to get away with driving, but yes, youngsters."

"And where the hell do kids get guns?" Kath said. "I know they do but if they're just kids…"

"Internet," said Vi. "You can get every bloody thing you want from the web."

"That's true and without more information, we haven't got a clue where to start," Jordan said. He looked at John.

John sighed. "Yeah, I know boss, get on to ballistics again."

Chapter 19

Benno pushed aside his *Helldivers* duvet. For a while, just last month, it had been his delight. Okay, asking for a computer game duvet cover was lame at his age, but he didn't need to tell anyone, and he liked it.

That was before. That was when guns and shooting games were all about fun and feeling clever, and being better than the other players. All before a woman died.

He slid out from under the covers and dragged his dressing gown over his sweatpants and T-shirt. First of all, he needed to speak to Stick, but his phone was downstairs plugged into the charger. He was going to be late getting to the yard again. Frank would be on his case. He sighed and kicked out at the laundry basket standing in the corner.

This wasn't what he'd expected to be doing. There had never been any pretence at school. He wasn't book clever. He was lazy, and he was disruptive. But that wasn't his fault. Of course he was disruptive, he had told his dad, he was bored. They weren't teaching him what he wanted to learn. When they asked what he wanted to learn, he had no answer. How was he supposed to know if they weren't teaching him? But sorting rubbish in his uncle's yard and driving a clapped-out white van wasn't how he'd imagined his adulthood to be.

It was okay for Stick; he was talented. Even Benno could see that, and he wanted to go to art college, and he probably would. Daz was different. He didn't need to be clever in school. He was just, well, just Daz. He had the street smarts. Somehow, he always had money, did what he wanted and turned up in the classroom now and again to keep in touch. Okay, he had it rough at home. His mam had got herself shacked up with some bloke who didn't think twice about giving Daz a clout round the ear just when he felt like it. But Daz wasn't bothered. At least he said he wasn't. Can't have been nice, though. And since his mam had the new baby, she'd written her older son off. Lost interest and was just waiting for the day when he left. So Daz roamed the streets, did some shoplifting and blagged drinks from old blokes in pubs who believed him when he said he was a refugee. He was good-looking, tall and slim with dark hair and brown eyes, and those daft accents he could put on, it worked with the duffers.

Benno glanced around the kitchen. There was nobody home. He slipped some waffles into the toaster and grabbed a couple of biscuits while he waited for the machine to pop. They had to find Daz. They had to get that money and replace their bikes before his mam and dad started asking questions.

He pulled a piece of paper from the pad by the landline telephone and tried to work out how much money there would be coming from the five thousand they had stashed. The sums wouldn't work, though. Dividing five thousand by three was too much for him without a calculator. It didn't matter. There had to be a lot. Probably wouldn't be enough to go off to London like Daz had planned, but it would be enough to buy the *Helldivers Dive Harder Edition* and a new bike. He couldn't get a better one because his younger brother would know and go whinging to his dad about wanting one himself, but with the computer game, they wouldn't know it wasn't the one he already had. He was always being told it was a waste of time spending hours and hours on the computer. Hadn't been a waste when they wanted to boost the cars, had it?

Computer lessons in school had been the biggest yawn. He was miles ahead of everyone else. That just worked for him. He could probably do something with that but didn't know how to even start. He couldn't write a CV and that was something you had to have, according to the careers teacher, and he didn't know how to tell her what he could do with a computer. She was too thick to understand. They all were. Didn't matter. Now, there was all this money. Probably spend some of it on new threads, some new trabs – Nike Air Max, they were well cool. He didn't know how much that would all cost, but if there was any left over, he'd put it away towards a car once he'd passed his test.

At the edge of his consciousness was the dead woman. He hadn't seen her in the post office, but now the news was putting pictures of her on the screen. She was just an old woman, somebody's mam, ordinary. He really wished

Daz hadn't hit her. Did he really need to have hit her? First thing he knew was when the other two dived in the car yelling at him to floor it and get away.

As he thought about it, the food he'd just eaten curdled in his stomach; he ran to the downstairs bathroom and threw up in the toilet bowl. He flopped backwards onto his backside in the corner and lowered his head onto his bent knees. He tried to stop the tears, but they came anyway. If only Daz hadn't hit that woman, it would still be a buzz. Just a laugh.

Benno wanted to ring Frank and say he couldn't come into work, but he needed to meet Stick. They had to find Daz. He needed the van.

He pushed up from the floor and went back into the kitchen. Now he'd have to have another waffle. He couldn't go to work with his stomach empty.

Chapter 20

With no bike, Benno had to take the bus and then walk to the yard. It made him get there even later, and Frank was livid when he arrived. So, he was out in the cold sorting wood panels when Stick rang him. He scuttered to the corner of the warehouse where the rain from the overhang dripped into a puddle of gritty grey water. He was cold and wet and dejected.

"The bizzies," Stick said. "Shit, man, the bizzies are here!"

"What the fuck, man? Where? Where are you?"

"I'm at the college. What should I do? I've tried to call Daz, but he's still not answering his phone. I'm bricking it. What should I do?"

"I don't know," Benno yelled into his phone. "I don't know what you should do. What did they say?"

"They didn't say nothing."

"How d'ya mean?"

"They didn't talk to me or nothing. I just saw them. They were out in the car park and then they came in and they were in the office. I'm in the art centre setting up my pictures and that, and I saw them through the window. I was gonna run, but the cop car's outside and I thought they might see me."

"Hang on, they didn't say nothing, and they just went in the car park?"

"Yeah."

"So, what are you panicking for, dork? They've been before, you know they have. They're always coming in, about drugs and knives and that. You don't know it's got anything to do with you. How long have they been there?"

"Dunno – half hour, maybe."

"And does everyone know you're there?"

"Well, the others do. The others in the exhibition and Mr Roberts, the art teacher."

"And nobody's come to talk to you?"

"No."

"So, just chill. It's probably nothing," Benno said.

"D'ya reckon?"

"Yeah. Just chill. Chill, man. Nobody knows it was us. Nobody knows nothing."

"They do though. They know about the bikes."

"What bikes?"

"The bikes, our bikes," Stick said.

"I haven't got no bike."

"Oh right, yeah, right."

"Okay. I'll see you later," Benno said.

"I can't, man," Stick said. "It's my mam's birthday. We're going out for a meal. It'll have to wait till tomorrow."

"Well, just keep your head down and don't worry, yeah?" Benno said. He stuffed his phone into his pocket and buried his face in his hands. He was right, wasn't he? The bizzies knew nothing. His gut gurgled again. He was going to get an ulcer if this went on. They had to find Daz.

Chapter 21

It was nearing the end of the shift, and the team gathered for the briefing. There were only negatives to report. No breakthrough from interviewing workers at the various industrial units near the hospital and no sightings of the bikes near the other crime scenes.

The trail was going cold and the other possibility, another robbery, just didn't bear thinking about. Stella had voiced the opinion that maybe they had been scared off by what had happened to Jean Court and, although they weren't making much headway, at least the chance of another post office raid was surely less than it might have been. There was a mutter of agreement and Jordan dismissed them.

Stella was collecting her coat and bag when her phone rang. She juggled with the handset wedged between her neck and shoulder as she clicked to turn off her computer and locked away her papers. Her eyes widened, and she held up a hand to alert the others.

"John, hang on," she said, stopping the DC in his tracks.

She lifted the phone away from her ear for a moment, telling whoever was at the other end to just wait. "The car, boss. I reckon we've found the blue Merc. No, that's not right, we've found where it was." She cancelled the shutdown of her laptop and asked the caller to come into the station as soon as possible.

The trip to the pub was forgotten as John and Jordan crowded around the computer, waiting for the footage to be sent through from the school. The uniformed officers were on the way with a copy on a thumb drive, but the CCTV video streamed from the school security showed the blue car entering the car park and pulling into a space in a corner behind the lines of vehicles.

They waited, and they watched as the time stamp ticked on, but although the headlights went out, nobody emerged from the car.

"Come on, come on," Stella said. "Get out, show yourselves, you bastards!"

But there was still no movement.

They zoomed in as close as they could, but it simply made the image pixilated and impossible to make out. "We need to get this to the technical department as soon as possible," Jordan said. "The car didn't drive itself into that corner, so one of them, at least, is still in there."

The incident room door opened, and a young constable stepped in beaming at them.

"Well done, officer. What can you tell us?" Jordan said.

"Okay." She glanced at the screen and then flipped open her notebook. "As you can see, the car parked up there early morning. I reckon it was just after the post office job. The time works with the timing of the robbery and the distance from Altway. I checked on Google maps on the way in."

Jordan murmured his approval, and she beamed wider.

"That's the good news. The not-so-good news is that nothing happens, not for a long time. A few hours go by. We've sent a copy of this to the techies already, but it just sits there. Nobody moves any of the cars around it. Then, when the school is closing, the car park gets busy with staff and a few of the older students collecting their vehicles. And the car moves off. Trouble is, there is such a lot of activity round about just then, that it will need to be viewed frame by frame to see if anybody actually gets into it or even looks into it, or interacts with anyone inside."

"It doesn't appear anyone got out, as far as we can see," John said.

"No, whoever was in it just stayed there. Further information is that the security bloke at the school didn't recognise the car, said he'd never seen it before. But that's not unusual because they have a lot of visitors and it's just one big parking lot. The only people with specific places are the heads of year who park near the doors."

"Of course they do," John muttered.

"Are there cameras at other parts of the school?" Jordan asked.

"One over the main door and three other entrances and the fire escape. We've asked for copies of the recordings. It's going to be a lot."

"So, what are you thinking?" Jordan asked the officer.

She took a moment to collect her thoughts. She hadn't expected to be questioned. "Okay, I read on the PNC reports and heard the alerts on the Airwaves that there were three people in the car when it drove away from the robbery, yes?" she said.

Jordan nodded.

"So, at some point two of the passengers got out of the car. They must have done. But there're people coming and going a lot of the time. It's sixth form, not like little kids who are supervised all day. It looked like nothing happened while it was parked up. We have all of that on CCTV. There were patrols everywhere so they weren't out in the road. But there are several entrances, especially if you include the emergency doors. My best guess is that two of them left the car and entered the school building and stayed there until they judged it was safe to drive to the hospital and hide themselves in the crush at visiting time. The driver hid himself in the vehicle and he did a bloody good job of it. It was pretty well planned in spite of the mess at the post office."

"Yes, and that went wrong for them because we picked them up with the ANPR. Great work, PC Taylor."

"Thank you, sir. Any chance I could be seconded to the team?"

"Blimey," John said. "Not backward at coming forward, are you, Sharon?"

"Don't get on by being a shrinking violet, do you, John?"

"I'll see what I can do," Jordan said, and the woman left the room and did a little victory dance in the corridor.

"I reckon she's most likely correct," Stella said. "It makes sense, that they probably went into the school. It would be an alibi for them. They would be able to move around freely and then leave when school finished. Jesus, that means that they must be schoolkids. No, can't be."

"The only other option is that they are staff," said Jordan. "Do you really see that?"

John muttered from the corner where he was making coffee, "Wouldn't put it past them."

"I guess you didn't like school much, John," Stella said.

"It was horrible. Couldn't wait to leave. It was only wanting to join the force that kept me there."

Stella leaned over and wrapped an arm around his shoulder. "And we're so glad you did, mate – mwah." She didn't kiss him, but the sound was enough to make him blush.

"Boss," John cried, "I've been assaulted."

Jordan grinned. This move forward had given them all a boost. Now they had to make it meaningful.

Chapter 22

When Frank came back from the betting shop, he had calmed down and brought Benno a couple of packets of crisps. "Listen, lad, I know you don't really see yourself here and I understand that," Frank said, "but you need to do better. You need to apply yourself. Decide which way you want to go."

"How d'ya mean, like? You're not sacking me, are you?"

"No, I'm not sacking you, but you worry me. If you want to carry on working in the yard, then you have to do better. You have to get here on time, work harder. But honestly, lad, you should be doing more. You can do all that stuff on the computer. Why don't you get yourself a job doing that? Make yourself some proper money, plan on moving out into your own place."

"Yeah, right. That's not going to happen any time soon. What's brought all this on, though?"

"We had the police in earlier," Frank said.

Bile rose in Benno's throat and the prawn cocktail flavoured snack he was swallowing threatened to come straight back up.

"The bizzies, what for?"

"They were just trying to track down some lowlife scum that'd robbed a post office and killed some poor old woman. They wanted to know if I'd seen anything of lads on bikes."

"What did you tell them?"

"I told them only the usual. Nobody new and nobody I didn't know. You didn't see anybody, did you? Monday it was. Oh no wait, you was at that college on Monday, wasn't you?"

"Yeah. All day. I didn't come here till really late."

"Aye, that's what I thought. Anyway, it made me think. You should sort yourself out. That skinny lad, what do you call him, Spit?"

"Stick, we call him Stick."

"Aye well, him, he's sorted, he's going to college with his drawing and that. You should try and do something like that, or you could end up like these scallies – going to the bad."

"No, I wouldn't do that, Uncle Frank. I wouldn't. God, how could you even say that?"

"Well, I'm just saying. Straighten up."

"I will, honest to God, I will. I'll stay late tonight if you like. Tidy up a bit more."

"Aye, go on then. But don't stay too late or I'll have your mam after me."

* * *

Once he was on his own again, Benno called Stick. "You okay?"

"Yeah. I'm out with my mam and dad. I told you."

"I know but I just wanted to make sure you were okay, and nothing had happened at school."

"Hang on a mo."

Benno heard Stick excuse himself, and the voice of his father as he snapped back about good manners and just a few hours with the family.

"I've got to be quick," Stick hissed through the phone.

In the background was the hubbub of a crowded restaurant. Benno craved the normality of it. He wanted to go back to the days when a trip to the carvery was the most excitement.

"I'll come tomorrow," Stick said. "Soon as I can, and we'll go and find Daz, and finish this."

"Yeah. We'll find Daz, get our money, and call a halt. It's horrible, is this. Not what it was supposed to be like," Benno said.

"We would never have done nothing like this if you hadn't found that gun, would we?" Stick said.

"Oh, so it's all my fault?"

"No, that's not what I mean. It's just that it was you finding it that gave Daz the idea."

"Yeah, but you went along with it, didn't you? You never said no. Anyway, I've got the van keys, and we'll find Daz."

"Where do you reckon he is? Not back at his house, not after last time."

"Well, where he stashed the money would be best. Up his granddad's allotment," Benno said.

"Okay. Listen, if he's not there, we'll grab the cash anyway. Not to rob him or nothing, just to have it and get us some new bikes and that."

"Yeah. Good idea. And if he is there, we'll tell him we're out of it now."

Chapter 23

The new information had encouraged the team, and they were all heads down viewing CCTV of the car park and the few private cameras from the route the Mercedes had taken. Now they knew they were looking for something specific, the job was easier.

The car was seen clearly twice, and the images were being enhanced as much as possible by the technicians. However, they could see from the first viewing that the driver and passengers had kept the face coverings on for the whole journey.

John and Jordan were at the school as the doors were unlocked at eight o'clock.

Their first conversation was with the maintenance supervisor who was unlocking the building. The man could not give them any information that they didn't already have. He hadn't noticed the blue car and as far as he was concerned, all the kids looked the same.

Once they had found him and been introduced, Brian Marsden, the headmaster, had stormed along the corridors, children pressing themselves against the walls as he passed. He admonished a couple, but Jordan was convinced it was for show and, as they followed to the administration suite, one of the boys gave the retreating head a two-fingered salute behind his back. Once in his office, there was no offer of tea or coffee, and Marsden seemed more concerned that there would be no liveried patrol cars on the school grounds for a second day running. He didn't want rumours to start and was sure, absolutely, that none of his students could be mixed up in armed robbery. The idea was ludicrous.

"And yet, the car was in your car park," John said.

"Doesn't prove anything really, though, does it?"

Jordan simply stared at him as they all registered how ridiculous that comment was.

"Okay, so what are you asking?" the head said.

"Is it possible to address the students?" Jordan said. "Maybe at assembly."

"Oh, Lord, we don't have assembly. The days of a hymn and a prayer are long gone. Only do that sort of thing on prize-giving day. No, if you want to talk to them, I could probably arrange a zoom address, but it's going to be very disruptive."

"It's pretty disruptive to turn up at work and have a gun shoved in your face, to be honest," John said.

The chilly atmosphere cooled a little more.

"To be more specific," Jordan said, "what we are looking for here are students who came in after the robbery had taken place. I can give you the timeline, including how long it would have taken them to cover the distance from the post office. Then, perhaps some of your staff could tell us if there was anyone that appeared agitated or over-excited?"

"We have older students in and out at different times of the day. We trust them to organise their own study time. You have to understand that teenagers are at a difficult stage in their development. What you might think is agitation we might see as enthusiasm. No, you are on the wrong track, Inspector. You should direct your enquiries elsewhere. I have raised this educational establishment from failing to outstanding in just three years and I won't have its name dragged through the mud. Bring me some proof and then we can talk further."

Jordan sighed. This was going nowhere. "We are going through the CCTV from the cameras over your entrances and exits. We are watching instant by instant the activity in the car park and if, or actually, I believe when, we spot our suspects among your student body, we will come back. When I write my report, I will ensure that it is known how helpful you've been." With that, he turned and left the room, with John close behind.

* * *

Jordan was still seething when they arrived back at Copy Lane. "We must find those lowlifes. They are something to do with the school and I'm looking forward to wiping that smug expression from the headmaster's face when we go back with images of them and their names."

He wrote up his report, frustrated that things weren't progressing faster. His irritation was interrupted by an excited yell from the office and he rushed in to see what had happened.

Kath had been viewing the CCTV from the college car park. The Mercedes had stopped at the gate because a car stalled in front of it and when the driver turned to look behind as he was forced to reverse, his face was revealed for a brief second. She made a note of the timing and called the technical department. Within a few minutes they had a still ready to send out to the media and put on posters for around the area. It was a huge move forward.

It had been a long day and Jordan still hadn't had a moment to call Pete at the hotel. Although they had a breakthrough, he still thought it was highly unlikely that he'd be able to have the weekend off apart from a couple of hours to shop for Harry's bed. He tried the mobile, and it went through to voicemail. He didn't want to cancel the arrangements over text or message, so he clicked off. There was still time.

Chapter 24

Benno was biting his nails and chewing at the inside of his bottom lip. He had spent the day trying to get on the good side of his uncle, who was still hanging around doing paperwork. The warehouse and break area were tidier than they had been in months.

Frank perched on the upright wooden chair in the corner, sipping on a can of lager and cursing the spreadsheet on his computer.

He flung the mouse across the table top. "I've had enough of this sodding thing. I'll have to get Margaret to do it," he said, referring to his wife, who normally had to pick up the slack as far as the book-keeping was concerned. "Come on, lad, let's go down the ale house and get us a bevvie."

Normally Benno would jump at the chance. He was still underage but in the company of a regular customer nobody was going to cause a fuss. Today, however, it was the last thing he wanted.

"I thought I might stop here a bit. I've got stuff to do on my computer."

"Oh well, you can do that at home, can't you?"

"Yeah, but your Wi-Fi is good here, and I thought I'd have a look at courses for college, while I'm in the mood, like. After what you said. Could be you've given me an idea? It'd be ace to get paid for messing with computers all day."

"Go on then. You can have a couple of cans if you like, seeing as you've put in a good shift. Lock up when you're done."

Frank pulled on his jacket, and moments later Benno heard his car reversing out of the yard. He texted Stick to meet him at the corner of the narrow road which passed the hospital. He switched off the lights and locked up, leaving a note for Frank explaining that he'd taken the van because he'd loaded it with rubbish for the tip and he would go there before work in the morning.

Stick was haggard and edgy, his head snapping back and forth as he peered along the road before clambering into the passenger seat.

"Up the allotment, yeah?" Benno said.

"Have you seen it?"

"Seen it? What, the allotment? 'Course I have. We've been loads of times. What you going on about?"

"No, not that." Stick held out his phone.

"Oh, shit." Benno swerved into the kerb and grabbed the handset. He clicked and scrolled as sweat broke out on his forehead and his stomach churned. The image of Daz was everywhere. The picture was blurry and pixelated, but anyone who knew him would easily recognise their mate.

"What we gonna do?" Stick said. "What the hell are we gonna do now?"

"Okay, look, don't panic." Benno clicked off the phone with trembling fingers. "It's not us. It's only Daz."

Stick stared at him in silence, his eyes wide, and his mouth gaping. "What!?"

"Like I say, it's not us. It's only Daz," Benno said.

"God, I don't believe you. What the hell difference does that make? They know the car was at the college. The pigs have been to the college. They say in the reports there were three people involved. Everyone who knows us knows we knock about with him. His mam knows."

"His mam's not going to dob him in, don't be thick," Benno said.

"Isn't she? How do you know that? If she doesn't, what about that shithead she lives with?"

"What do you think we should do, then? We don't know where he is. Wherever he is, he must have seen this. It'll be on his phone."

"We should go up the allotment," Stick said, nodding his head. "Yeah. Let's do that. I bet he'll be there."

"Why do you think that?"

"Because, soft lad, that's where the money is. He's gonna have to do a runner, isn't he? No way he can stay round here. So, he'll need money. It might already be too late."

"Too late for what?" Benno said.

"For us, if he's gone up there, he'll have taken the lot. He won't have left any behind."

"Oh, fuck."

Chapter 25

Only two of the six civilian clerks had gone home. They didn't want to and apologised, but Jordan did his best to reassure them. "You've worked a full day. We're pretty well covered," he told them as he looked around the room.

Kath had her head down in front of the computer. Stella was on the phone, as were the remaining civilians. Vi was collating the reports coming in. Sharon Taylor had joined the team after a day in the patrol car and was taking calls with the rest of them. Jordan smiled across the room at her, and she blushed and lowered her gaze.

It had been non-stop since the image had been published and their time was taken with weeding the useless, the mischievous and the plain stupid from any calls that might just tell them who the driver of the Mercedes was.

Jordan had tried several times to contact the headmaster of the school, but he was either deliberately avoiding contact or genuinely unavailable. If they didn't reach him, then he was going to receive another visit in the morning and Jordan would insist that they have access to all the staff and students. Someone there knew who this bloke was. It was always possible that he was not a student at the school, but realistically, that was unlikely.

They believed he had dropped the other two suspects off to enter the building; another hypothesis was that two of them had left to go elsewhere, and he was simply waiting to meet up with them for the final run to the hospital car park when things were calmer and it was safe to collect their bikes.

Jordan was convinced they were in the school and once they had the name of this one, it would surely take them straight to the other two. He knew from his own youth that lads roam in gangs. You find one and you wheedle out the rest.

He had called Penny and told her he was going to be late and not to wait for him to eat. He had tried again to call Pete, but still the phone went to voicemail.

"Are you going to show the picture to Jean's family?" Stella asked.

"No," Jordan said. "Honestly, I reckon they must have seen it anyway, and until we find him, we don't have much to tell them. What I really don't want to do is wind up the son and have him out roaming the streets again. It might well happen and there's not much we can do unless he makes a nuisance of himself. I sympathise, I really do, but I think we just tread carefully. If they contact us and ask, we tell them he's a person of interest. I've already had a patrol speak to Lilian Goudy, who is back in the shop now, but she didn't recognise him."

When the call came, John took it. The school maintenance supervisor was reticent and nervous. He identified himself and let them know, though he was sure he recognised the driver, he couldn't really remember his name and there was no way he was attending any identity parades or such like or going to court.

"So," John said, "what can you tell me, mate?"

"He was at the school. He always caused trouble when he was younger, and I don't know what he's hanging around for now. He only comes in a few times a term, pretty irregular, and when he does, he just loiters in the corridors or the dining room. I'm sorry I've been trying to remember his name, but there's hundreds of them in that place. He might not even be registered anymore, but that's not my responsibility. I reckon his real name was something like Dennis or Derek. Anyway, everyone called him Dazzy or Dizzy, something like that."

"Do you know where he lives?"

"Nah, that's not my job, is it? I just clean up after the buggers. I don't suppose I've been much help."

"On the contrary, at least now we know for sure he was a student there and we most likely have his nickname. That's a great help. Thank you so much."

Stella pushed back from her desk and stretched. From the table in the corner, she waved the coffee pot. Jordan nodded and gave her a thumbs-up.

"Have you had a chance to read the report about the gun?" she said as she handed him the mug.

"No, didn't see it had come in. Hang on." Jordan scrolled through his messages. "Ah, got it." He was quiet for a few minutes, sipping at the coffee and squinting at the screen.

"Looks like you need your eyes tested, boss," Stella said, grinning at him.

"I know, I do. When do I have time? I wonder how I'll look with glasses."

"You'll look cool. Of course you will."

Jordan glanced up and gave her a quick smile. She blushed.

"Well, that's odd, isn't it?" he said as he swivelled away from the desk.

"Yeah, do you mean the notes at the end? It says it's a preliminary report and there will be more when they've analysed the test firing and what not. But whoever was looking at it was just as intrigued as we were."

"You'd probably expect oil residue," said Jordan, "but it should be gun oil, not sunflower oil, surely. Then there's that about woollen threads and vegetable matter. What on earth is that? Vegetable matter? Put a copy of this on the board. It's odd, and they haven't come up with any reasoning, just facts. Probably because they don't want to risk being wrong."

Stella put the printout on the board.

"When you have a chance, guys," Jordan said, "have a look at that and see what you can make of it."

There was a buzz as the team read the report. There was discussion and then someone laughed.

"Boss," John said, "Sharon had an idea." He turned. "Go on, girl, tell him."

The young officer was pink and flustered. "Sorry, boss," she began.

Jordan had turned to look at her and he raised his eyebrows and waited.

"PC Sharon Taylor, boss. Sorry, it's just that the description made me remember a time when I had to fish my ASP out of a skip. Some moron had grabbed it and flung it in. I had to actually climb in and root around for it. It came up covered in shit; so did I, actually. Of course I'd gone on my arse when I climbed in. Honest to God, there was stuff all over me. Well, not shit exactly, but crap like this. Oil and sticking to the oil was old bits of rag and in the little joints there was, like, you know, food and that. Bits of chips and lettuce. I had bread buns stuck to my feet."

By now, most of the officers were struggling to hold back the laughter and Jordan was fighting to keep his expression serious. Sharon glanced around and went even pinker.

"All as I'm saying," she continued, "is that to get covered in that stuff just go into a skip."

"What happened to the scally?" someone asked.

"Oh, I'd kneed him in the goolies. He was already locked in the back of the police van." There was a cheer at this, and she flapped her hand at them. "What I'm saying is that maybe the gun had been in a skip, you know, a skip or a bin, or on the tip." The laughter fizzled out, and she looked round at the faces in the room.

"Well done, Sharon. That's what this is all about. The gun's been thrown away. So, either these lads found it or someone else did and they've sold it on," John said.

"Yeah, but not someone who knows about guns. Nobody who was used to guns would leave it like that. They would have dismantled it and cleaned it up. It says that it wasn't loaded, but we knew that because it was checked immediately. Maybe it never was. Maybe they found a discarded weapon and saw that it would scare people. Sharon, you're a star," Stella said as she high-fived the other woman.

Chapter 26

The rain had stopped. Grey streaks of cloud smeared across the darkening blue of the sky. As the last of the light faded, a waning gibbous moon crept up over Manchester and Benno drove out towards Kirkby and the allotment.

"What are you gonna say to him?" Stick asked.

"Just that we want our share of the money."

"What if he asks us to do a bunk with him?"

"I'll just tell him, no. What about you?"

Stick sniffed and blew his nose into a raggy piece of kitchen roll.

Benno glanced at him and saw the glint of liquid in his eyes. He understood the fear.

"We'll help him," Benno said. "He's a mate, but that's all. I'm not going off somewhere. He already said there isn't enough money for London, so what's he going to do? I'm not going to sleep in no doorway or nothing. I'm just going to keep my head down and wait while this all goes away."

"How are we gonna help him, though?" Stick said.

"Oh, for fuck's sake, Stick, shut up. I don't know, right. I don't bloody know. Let's just see if he's there first."

The allotments were behind a metal fence, and the gates were padlocked. This presented no problem for the two lads, who parked the van under the trees at the side of the road and scrambled over the railings in the dark.

It was quiet save for the shush of wind in the trees and the skitter of tiny creatures alarmed by their passing feet.

"Down the end. That one with the shed and the plastic tunnel thing," Benno said.

He had brought the torch from the van and the white cone of light glinted on the lying water from the earlier rain.

"Be quiet, moron," he said as Stick splashed through the puddles.

"Why?"

"Well, in case he's there."

"But we're gonna talk to him, aren't we?" Stick asked.

Benno stopped and turned to shine the torch into his friend's face. "Well, yeah, we are, like, but I just wanted to have a look first of all. See if he's there and that."

"What if he's not there?"

"We'll grab the money," said Benno. "I think that's best. I know the old fella doesn't come up here much, but I reckon we're better off having it with us."

"Why?" Stick asked.

"Jesus, so that if he gets caught, we'll have the money." As he spoke, Benno reached out and jabbed Stick's forehead with his finger. "Think, you pillock. Just think. The filth are looking for him. I know we're not going to dob him in or nothing, but who knows? They might catch him and if they do, chances are they'll search everywhere. They'll look here. So, we take the money now and keep it safe."

"You've thought this all out, haven't you?"

"Good job one of us has, innit."

They walked off the path and onto the narrow allotment plot and high-stepped over the wet grass and weeds. Benno led the way across the lumpy soil to the polytunnel at the other end of the space.

The plastic shelter was quite a few years old and beginning to turn brittle. The zip holding the roll-up door caught and snagged as Benno pulled it upwards. He made a hole large enough to squeeze through to the inside.

"Shit man, you've wrecked it," Stick said.

"So what? Let's just get the bag and go. He put it in the water butt in the corner."

"It'll be wet."

"There's no water in it, duh brain. He uses it to store old sacks and plant pots and crap. Bring me that crate so I can reach. Hold the torch."

Benno leaned his belly on the edge of the plastic barrel and hung his head down inside. "Get the torch over here."

"Hang on. I need something to stand on." Stick dragged a plastic box across the gritty floor and, holding the torch wedged between his neck and shoulder, he shuffled it into place and stepped up.

"I can't see it. It's a big grey bag, with a zip on the top. Yellow handles. Can you see it?" Benno's voice was breathy and strained as he leaned further and further into the water butt.

They didn't hear the rattle of the plastic and the soil floor swallowed the sound of footsteps.

"Is this what you're looking for, lads?"

Chapter 27

The headmaster had managed to avoid the phone calls and had hoped to avoid a reception committee when he arrived at the school just after seven on Friday morning. As he made much of retrieving his briefcase from inside the car and throwing his raincoat onto the back seat, Jordan and Stella walked across the parking space to stand close to the rear of the vehicle. He glanced up at them and sighed.

"Good morning, Mr Marsden. You'll have seen the pictures in the media, I expect," Jordan said.

"I have."

"We need his name and any other details you have. We need to know who he spent his time with. I'm sure you want to get this over with quickly and quietly."

"I haven't confirmed that he was a student here."

"Oh, come on," Stella said, "how thick do you think we are? We haven't got time to waste. We know he was one of yours and you know he was, so let's just get this done."

The filing cabinets were in a room alongside the headmaster's office. It didn't take long for him to retrieve the file.

"Daniel Burdon. His friends called him Daz. I'll write down his address. The home situation is not perfect."

"How do you mean?" Jordan asked.

"His father left quite some time ago. There is some contact with a grandfather. However, he lives with his mother who has a new man in her life. Daniel and the new man don't get on. I think there may be abuse of a sort, but Daniel hasn't complained officially to anyone here."

"So, you didn't do anything about it?" Stella said.

The headmaster shrugged. "We're limited as to how much we can interfere."

"Balls." Stella didn't hide her disgust. "You are responsible for these kids. You think he might be ill-treated and you can't do anything?"

Jordan turned and raised his eyebrows. He understood, but now was not the time. They needed to find the boy and it would be someone else's responsibility to decide how much his home situation had contributed to how he'd turned out.

"We need to know about his close friends. Pictures and address details, if you have them," Jordan said.

By the time Jordan and Stella had all the information, the school had come alive. They pushed through the swarm of pupils milling about the corridors and on the stairs. The car park was full and the road outside busy with people dropping off their children.

"God, this brings back memories," Stella said. "I didn't hate school, not like John, but I didn't love it either. Wouldn't want to go back."

"I didn't mind it," Jordan said. "Actually, when that old school friend got in touch, I was surprised how nice it felt to meet someone from back then."

As Jordan drove them away, Stella put the names and details of the three boys into the computer. None of them had a police record.

"Daniel Burdon's house first, I think," Jordan said. "In the meantime, arrange to have the new images published with a 'Do you know these people?' request. Could be we'll have them by the end of the day."

* * *

It was still early when Stella and Jordan arrived at the Burdons' house in Aintree. The curtains were opened and as they arrived, a tall, middle-aged man stepped through the door. He was dressed for work in blue overalls, but he carried a small leather case. The headlights on a Renault Megan blinked and by the time he had stowed the bag, Jordan and Stella were alongside with their warrant cards held out for him to see.

"Didn't take you long," the man said, "though in fairness, I expected you last night."

"You know why we're here?" Stella said.

"Well, I haven't been done for speeding lately and I don't think illegal parking gets the attention of detectives, so it's that waste of skin, Daniel."

"You saw the appeal for information?" Jordan asked.

"Aye."

"You didn't come forward."

"Don't be so bloody daft. I might think he's a no mark, but he's my bird's kid. She might be just waiting till he gets old enough to bugger off, but he's her son when all's said and done. It didn't give much detail on the web. A serious crime, it said. So, go on then, what's he supposed to have done?"

"Do you have any idea where he might be, Mr…"

"Hastings, John." He pointed to a small sticker on the car door. "That's me, Hastings Electric. My own business, four employees now. Taken me years to get it going, get myself a reputation and I'm not having that scrote ruin it for me. He's not mine. I've tried to knock him into shape, but he won't change. I wouldn't care if I never saw him again. So, no, I don't know where he is. No idea. Haven't seen him since last Tuesday."

The officers saw him put two and two together. He frowned and shook his head.

"Nah. He wasn't involved in that thing on Monday, was he?"

"Which thing?" Stella said.

"That robbery up on Altway. Held me up for ages, it did. But come on, that was supposed to be an armed robbery. You can't imagine for a minute he had anything to do with that. He's a kid. He's not even properly left school yet. Not that he goes much. I've tried to tell him. If he wants to get on, he has to put in the work, but he's a lost cause, if you ask me."

"We can't get into details at this point, especially as you're not a relation, but if you know where he might be, it would be best if you tell us now."

"Okay, if you're going to be like that, you best speak to his mam."

John Hastings pointed towards the front of the house and the woman in the doorway, who was dressed in a thick dressing gown and jigging a baby on her hip.

Jackie Burdon didn't offer them coffee. They stood in the hallway while she soothed her baby by rocking the stroller back and forth. Nervous but doing her best to keep herself under control, she confirmed she hadn't seen her son since Tuesday.

"Do you know where his friends might be?"

"No, Stick might be at school. He wants to get into college. The other one, God knows."

Jordan jotted down some notes in his book, and they turned to leave. "If you hear from your boy, let us know. Better still, ask him to come in and speak to us. We can sort all this out. The longer it takes to find him, the more complicated it becomes," he said.

* * *

Stella drove Jordan's Golf as he checked the overnight reports. She clicked the hands-free button on the steering wheel when his phone rang.

Jordan gave John an update and told him they were heading back.

"Got a possible identification from some old lady in Netherton," John said. "Might be nothing, but I wonder if it's worthwhile you calling in to see her. It's not far out of your way."

They noted the address and headed along Dunnings Bridge Road towards Park Lane.

Mrs Jenny Milford wasn't as old as John had suggested. Probably early seventies and still well turned out and lively. This time, they got coffee and a thick slice of malt loaf loaded with butter. They were ready for the sugar boost. She was proud of her new kitchen, very proud, and clicked open cupboards and switched on cabinet lights to show them. They didn't have the time for it, but she lived alone, and they didn't have the heart to hustle her along.

Back in the living room, Mrs Milford settled in her chair. "So, I had this cooker taken out. It was too good to throw away really, but I couldn't get anybody to buy it. The Salvation Army couldn't take it because it was electric. Load of nonsense when there's people needing stuff. Anyway, in the end I had to give it to the scrap man. That's when I saw those lads. Came in a van and trampled all over my garden. Late at night bothering people."

"And you think it was the young men in the pictures?" Jordan said.

"Oh, yes, it was them. Tried to hide their faces, they did. Silly sods. Must think I'm doolally. I'm not and when people come round my place, especially at night, I have them on my security camera. You can't see it because I had it hidden under the eaves. It's not to scare people off, it's to see what's going on – birds and what have you – but it's good for when the delivery men come as well. Anyway, I've downloaded the recording and put it on a memory stick for you. I lifted screen shots of a couple of the clearer images of their faces and zoomed in as far as I could to get a good picture. I've put the scrap man's contact details on there as well. His phone and email and his address. Oh yes, mine is there in case you need to speak to me again."

There was a moment of silence. Jordan and Stella glanced at each other. Mrs Milford laughed.

"And don't be calling me a silver surfer either. I've been using computers since the ZX80 and you won't even know what they are. Electronics and computers have been my life since I was a young woman. Here, finish your drink and then let me get on."

She handed over the thumb drive.

Chapter 28

The M6 in Lancashire is never quiet. It is very rare for there to be an empty stretch.

Benno hadn't any experience of motorway driving. It was something that had to wait until he passed his test. Now in among the streaming traffic, his knuckles were white as he gripped the wheel of the old van rattling along on the inside lane. Sweat beaded on his forehead, but he didn't dare raise his hand to brush it aside.

"Can't you go any faster?" Daz growled.

"But, Daz, it's an old van. It's clapped out and not meant for this. This is scary, all these great big lorries flashing their lights at me."

"That's because you're in their way. They're telling you to get a shift on."

"I know, but I've never done this before. If you're so bloody clever, why don't you do it?"

Benno regretted the words as they left his lips. The big knife that had been tucked into Daz's belt rested on his lap. Now he picked it up, leaned across the cab and poked the point into Benno's neck, the sharp end drawing a bead of blood.

"I will, fatso," Daz said viciously. "Next services you'll shove over, and I'll drive."

"You can't drive."

"I can do better than you. Anyway, how hard can it be?"

"It's not the same as *Grand Theft Auto*, and Frank's going to be really pissed off if we smash his van up."

"Frank! Do you actually think I give a fuck what Frank thinks? This is bigger than Frank. This is serious real-world stuff. This is epic, man."

"Where are we going, Daz, and what are we going to do about Stick? He's not looking good."

"I haven't decided yet and Stick's fine. He's gonna have a headache, is all. It's his own fault. He should have done as he was told."

"There was no need to hit him, though. You scared us creeping in like that."

"I told him to stand still. He didn't stand still. Let that be a lesson to you, Benno. Best if you do as I tell you, yeah?"

Daz turned in the seat to peer at Stick, slumped in the back with his eyes closed. There was a thin track of blood down the side of his face, but it was crusting now, and his cheek was beginning to show the colour of a deep bruise.

"I thought we were mates. I thought we were in this together," Benno said.

"Yeah, so why were you trying to nick my money?"

"We wasn't. I said already, we were looking for you and then when you weren't there, we were just gonna put it somewhere safe. I told you."

"Stop whining. Just get us up to Charnock Richard, then we'll boost a decent car and leave this junk heap in the car park."

Chapter 29

Jordan streamed the video from Mrs Milford to all the screens in the incident room. The close-up images of the lad's faces had already been printed out and mounted on the whiteboard.

"She did a brilliant job, that woman," Kath said. "It's a damn shame she couldn't get a view of the licence plate."

"It doesn't matter, though," Jordan said. "She's given us the address of the scrapyard and Stella and I are on our way there now. I just wanted to bring this in, so you were all up to date."

Vi raised her hand. "Boss, I've seen that van."

"Where?"

"I've seen it at the other scenes of the burned-out cars." She consulted her notes, clicked and scrolled through the videos, stopping and zooming in. "That's it, isn't it? See that patch of rust under the door? I'm sure that's it."

Jordan leaned in to look more closely at the screen.

"Yeah, that's it. Well done. So, that's more proof that we're getting this right. Many thanks to Mrs Milford, it has to be said. We need to find it now. As soon as we have the registration number from this Frank person, I'll send it through. This is brilliant stuff, guys. We're getting there."

* * *

Frank had only just arrived in his yard. He'd put on the kettle and taken out the paper bag holding his cinnamon roll. This was the best part of the day. Elevenses, away from his wife and her nagging about money, holidays and shopping, and before he had to get out to do collections. He was irritated to find his van wasn't there, but at least he had some time on his own before Ben came back. The note on the table explained it, and he could use the little flatbed lorry for the morning. He'd ring his idle nephew in a while if he hadn't turned up. He'd need the van later for the afternoon trawl. It was more manageable around the narrower roads on the estates and it had the big horn to let people know he was in the area.

There was the sound of a car engine, but he knew immediately that it wasn't Ben. He sighed and stuck a woollen cosy over the little brown teapot.

A VW Golf had pulled into the car entrance, and it was obvious right away that the two figures crossing the yard were bizzies. It was something to do with the way they walked, the confidence.

He did a mental rundown of everything he'd collected in the last few days. There was nothing dodgy as far as he could remember. Mind, these days you could never tell. Everybody was up to something. They were just trying to get by, but the law didn't often see it like that. There'd been no lead flashing that could have come from a roof; nothing that seemed off, just the usual – old bike frames, clapped-out cookers and rusted, dented sinks. No, nothing to worry about, so he pasted a smile on his face and went to meet them with his hand out, ready for a friendly greeting. No point antagonizing the force.

* * *

Frank showed Jordan and Stella the note the lad had left. It would have been better if he could speak to the stupid sod first and make sure there was nothing going on that he needed to know about. They insisted they needed his mobile phone number, his address, and when he was last seen.

He wondered if the lad had been picked up for speeding or something; it could see him banned for years, not to mention screwing up the insurance. That wasn't going to please his sister or his wife.

Frank wished now that he hadn't shown them the note, he could have played dumb and left them with more work to do. Maybe he could blag his way out of it.

"Is this about him driving the van? I've told him to always make sure he has a qualified driver with him. One of his mates, if it's not me."

"Which mates would they be?" Jordan asked.

"Oh, whichever one is with him?"

"Would one of those mates be Daniel Burdon?"

"If that's Daz, yes, he's one of them."

"According to our records, Daniel doesn't have a licence of any sort."

"Ah, no. What I mean is, more than likely he would be with them, like, but one of the others."

"Who else might be with him?"

Frank was rapidly finding himself out of his depth, and the longer this went on, the more complicated it would be to back-pedal.

"Of course, I didn't see him last night. That's why he left the note, see? I can't say for certain who he'd be with."

"So, you don't know where he is right now?"

"He'll be at home, I suppose. Not what you call an early riser, isn't Benno – that's what they call him, Benno. His proper name is Benjamin, but it's a bit of a mouthful for most people." Frank tried a laugh, but there was no response. He cleared his throat. "Then again, he might be at the tip or between the two."

They asked for the licence number, MOT, and insurance details, and Frank sent up a short prayer of thanks that everything was up to date.

"If he comes here, could you give me a ring right away?" Jordan said.

"Yeah, yeah, of course. Is he in trouble?"

"We need to have a word and then we'll see," Stella said.

After they left, Frank called his sister. She'd had a message to say he was with Stick and Daz, and it didn't say where they were headed. She insisted she wasn't concerned, but there was something in her voice to contradict her words. Frank called his nephew several times and there was no response. He left messages. Suddenly the cinnamon roll didn't seem so appetizing. There was a worm of worry squirming in his gut. What had the stupid arse done now?

On the way back to the station, Stella arranged to have the details sent to all the patrols and on the PNC. If the van was on the road, it wouldn't be long before it was seen.

Chapter 30

Benno had loved motorway services ever since he'd been a kid. There was everything there that he liked. Shops full of sweets and fizzy drinks, fast-food places with chips and burgers, and usually a game zone with the latest games. Today, though, it was all wrong.

Daz had made him park the white van in among the huge lorries to hide it. Then when they'd gone over to the services building, they'd left Stick in the back. He looked horrible. Daz said he was just sleeping off his headache, but when Benno shook his shoulders, the only reaction had been a dull groan.

"We'll bring him some water back. He'll be sound. Come on, I need a pee and we need to scope out a car."

Benno had tried to tell him he didn't have any idea how to nick a car without the computer set-up that was on the tablet in his bedroom at home. That only worked with the most recent cars, the ones that didn't have actual keys. Daz was talking about hotwiring a ride and Benno thought he was away with the fairies.

They visited the gents and then picked up burgers and coffee to go, and bottles of water.

"Better get some butties for later. We don't know how long we're gonna be on the road," Daz said.

So, they went into the supermarket for crisps and snacks. It would have been fun if it hadn't been for the state of Stick, the dead woman, the sneaking suspicion that this was all going to go horribly wrong, and that, despite his bravado, Daz didn't really have a plan.

Daz was jumpy and hyper, his eyes were wild and when he paid in the shop, his fingers were quivering. Benno didn't think he was on anything, but how could he know for sure?

They ate the burgers sitting at one of the outside tables near the entrance. Daz insisted they should watch for a car to nick. But Benno wasn't sure what he was supposed to be looking for. He had repeated that he didn't know how you started an engine without the key and Daz shook his head and tutted. After a while, he screwed up the food wrapper and threw it towards one of the bins, where it landed on the ground in a greasy puddle.

"Okay, I know what we're going to do," Daz said.

"What about Stick?"

"I reckon we'll leave him in the back of the van. It'll be better than trying to cart him with us."

"But he might need a doctor or the ozzy."

"Yeah, well, somebody'll find him, won't they? Or he'll get out when he wakes up and get himself a lift home."

It was heartless, and Benno felt really scared for the first time. "No, let's take the van and forget about nicking a car. Where are we going, anyway?" he said.

Daz sighed. "Listen, bird brain. That clapped-out heap of junk is too slow. I want something better. We're going up to the Lakes. It's a couple of hours and I don't want to be knackered when we get there."

"Why are we going there?"

"I know a place we can stay for a bit. My old fella's mate has a caravan. I know where he stows the key for people who rent it. We'll get some scran, some booze, it'll be the gear, like a holiday. But first, we'll get a car."

"I need to go to the bog again," Benno said.

"You've just been."

"Yeah, well, my guts are rotten. It's all the stress."

"God, you're like an old tart. Go on then. Hurry up. I'll meet you back at the van. We need to grab the bag and then I know how we can get wheels. This is brilliant, is this. This is living. Come on, don't get a cob on, loosen up."

In the cubicle in the gents, Benno could hardly see for the tears, and his fingers dithered on the keyboard as he typed a text to his uncle.

> *In big trouble. Sticks in a bad way.*
> *Charnock Richard in your van.*

He pushed the phone back into his pocket and went through the sales hall, the smell of hot grease turning his stomach.

Daz stood beside one of the great juggernaut lorries with the money bag in his hand. He handed it over to Benno.

"Bloody hell, what have you got in here? It weighs a ton. I thought this was the money."

"It is, but it's got my stuff in it. I wasn't leaving my good stuff for that arse at Mam's. Stop whining, look." He pointed at a grey Ford Focus. "See that? That's our car."

"How d'ya mean, like?" Benno said.

"It's an old bloke on his own. He's got a stick to walk, and he looks like he might not make it to the bogs in time."

Benno couldn't see the old bloke. "Where is he?"

"Gone in the services. So, keep an eye out and stay close. We have to move fast." As he walked away, Daz pulled the knife from the waistband of his trousers.

"Daz, wait on. What are you going to do? Let's not, let's just take the van."

Daz spun on his heels, his face reddening, his eyes flashing. "For the last time, we're not taking the bloody van. We're going to take this. Okay, it's still a piece of junk, but it's a better piece of junk. Since you haven't got the nous to nick something decent, I'll have to do it myself. So, stay close, keep an eye out, and be ready."

Chapter 31

The front desk at Copy Lane was manned by civilian receptionists. Tracy was in her first week. She was supervised by Glenda, who was close to retiring. Neither of them was to blame, or maybe both of them were. Tracy didn't know what to do and Glenda had needed the loo.

When Frank brought in his note and told Tracy that it should be given right away to 'the big, coloured bloke who was in charge of the post office case', she didn't know who he meant. She intended to tell Glenda and, if the drunk woman who had lost her handbag and the two teenagers who thought the woman living next door was a witch and should be arrested hadn't arrived noisily together, then she would have.

After an hour dealing with the time-wasting witch finders and calming the woman, who would probably never see her handbag again, they both needed a cup of tea. Tracy brought the mugs from the back room and shifted some paperwork to make room on the desk. That was when she remembered.

"Oh shit! Sorry, Glen. I should have told you about this. Some bloke came in with a note for whoever is dealing with the post office robberies. I didn't know who that was."

"It's that lovely Inspector Carr, the one who brings donuts. I'll take it up to him. It wasn't urgent, was it?" As she spoke, she unfolded the piece of paper. "Oh, bugger, he should have had this. It's about where the van is. That van, the one that everyone's been looking for. The one with the lads on the website and everything."

Glenda placed her mug on the edge of the desk. It toppled onto the floor, splashing onto Tracy's new high tops and up her trouser legs.

"Am I in trouble?" she called, as Glenda disappeared through the door into the rest of the building.

"I reckon we both might be, love. But it's my fault for leaving you."

* * *

Jordan could have read the Riot Act, he could have raged and complained, but what would be the point? He looked at the note and before Glenda slunk back to reception, he was on the way out of the incident room, dragging on his jacket, calling for John and Stella to meet him in the car park.

They took Jordan's car. Stella's electric vehicle was charging, and John's was a rust box, which he was saving hard to replace. It was quicker than signing out a pool car.

They got on the M58, joining the M6 at Orrel, heading towards Preston. Stella read the note out loud to John and then over Airwave to the traffic officers. It was basically a copy of the text message Benno had sent, with the added information that Frank was heading up to the services and he was going to have his nephew's guts for garters when he laid his hands on him. John contacted Lancashire Constabulary to let them know what was going on.

The van had been found by the time the team from Liverpool arrived at Charnock Richard. An ambulance stood in the parking area among the lorries. The door was open, and a gurney stood alongside the Transit's side door. Frank was there, pacing back and forth and swearing. As Jordan approached, he flung the remainder of a cigarette onto the floor and ground it to dust with the heel of his boot.

"You took yer time," he growled.

"Sorry, your message didn't get to me as soon as it should. Who is in there?" Jordan pointed to the van.

"It's that kid they call Stick. They won't let me in, they were here before me. They've been in there with him for a bit. Took some stuff in and wouldn't say nothing. Was it you who called them?"

"Yes, we did, on the strength of your message."

"Right. I had hoped maybe it'd been Ben who rang them. Doing the right thing for once."

"I don't suppose your nephew is here?"

"No, he's not, nor that bloody Daz either."

Stella had already gone into the services building to find the security officer and arrange access to the CCTV.

"Have you tried ringing him?"

"Of course I have. His phone's off now or the batteries flat or something. There's no answer. I've been all over here, and I can't find him. The other cops have seen a picture of him and they're looking, but I don't know where he's gone."

Jordan put a hand on the other man's shoulder. In spite of his rough exterior and gruff attitude, he was distressed and worried.

"We'll find him," Jordan said. "And when we do, we can sort all this out."

"Aye. I wonder where that'll leave us. I tried to help him, to guide him. But I've done no good, have I?"

"Let's just find him first, eh?" Jordan said.

Jordan moved to the rear of the white van and peered inside. The paramedics were heads down, concentrating on their patient. He didn't want to disturb them right then. The lad was in good hands. He turned away to head for the security office as a second ambulance came to a halt near the entrance.

"We don't need that, do we?" Jordan asked the traffic officer, who was in charge of the scene.

"No, that's something else. Some old bloke has had a heart attack. Told the woman on the counter near the door that he was attacked in the car park by two lads with a big knife. Said he had his car nicked. Then he went down like a sack of spuds. What a bloody day this has turned out to be."

He had barely finished with his complaint before Jordan was striding across the tarmac towards the emergency vehicle.

Inside the services there was a huddle of people, one of whom was kneeling on the floor with the mobile defibrillator case open beside him. The figure of an old man was in the recovery position, but the attendant was talking to him and nodding at the answers. Jordan took out his warrant card and kneeled on the tiles.

"How is he doing?" he asked the first-aider.

"Seems stable right now, but it was touch and go there for a while. I'll be glad to hand him over to these guys." He waved a hand toward the paramedics.

"Any chance I could have a quick word?"

"Bit off, mate. I mean, he's in pain and shocked. Can't it wait?"

"Yes, of course, if you don't think he's up to it."

"Well, not my decision now." With that, the man turned to give the report of what he'd done and what the old man's situation was. "I'll leave you with these fine gentlemen, Mr Hargreaves," he said. Then, the first-aider leaned over and patted his patient on the arm. He glared at Jordan, who was leaning close to the man's ear, and tutted as he began to tidy up his equipment.

"Mr Hargreaves, don't exert yourself but can you tell me what happened?"

"Come on, chum, out the way." The paramedic pushed Jordan aside as he leaned in to wrap a blood pressure cuff around the skinny, flabby arm.

Hargreaves muttered quietly and gripped Jordan's hand with weak, sweaty fingers.

"Two lads," he gasped. "Had a knife, bastards. Get my car back, mate." With this pathetic request, Mr Hargreaves gave himself over to the attention of the paramedics and whatever came next.

Stella was beside Jordan now and he asked her to go in the ambulance so she could interview Mr Hargreaves as soon as it was safe. "If you can get a description, that'd be excellent. But I reckon it's Benno and Daz. Do your best to get the make and registration as quick as you can. In the meantime, John and I will look at the security cover of the car park. We might be lucky."

"Yeah, no probs, boss. Only thing is, how am I going to get home?"

"I promise I'll either pick you up or send a patrol car."

"Okay, only I don't want to end up on a train in the middle of the night."

"No, you won't. Scout's honour." He raised a hand in a mock salute.

Chapter 32

Benno wanted out. He was scared and upset. Watching Daz threaten the old man with his knife and then push him into the bushes and leave him floundering and frightened had been horrible. When Daz yelled at him to grab the keys and get in the car, he had done it because he couldn't see a way not to. There was the knife, there was the old man moaning and there was Daz yelling, while all he wanted was to be somewhere else.

He no longer recognised his friend. He had always been a bit on the wild side. That had been part of the attraction. Benno knew he was dull, not attractive to the girls and not talented like Stick. But running with the other two, he felt their kudos rubbed off on him and made life more exciting. Now, it wasn't exciting. It was vicious and scary. He couldn't convince himself that, if push came to shove, Daz wouldn't hurt him.

The car didn't have a sat nav and Daz was using Google on the phone he'd snatched from the old man for directions. He'd insisted Benno turn his off to avoid it being traced. He'd done the same with his own.

"That old bloke won't even be able to remember his number. They never can, those old codgers, so we can use this for now and then we'll get a burner if we need one."

Up to now, it had been easy. Straight up the motorway. The traffic was still busy, but this car was easier to drive than the lumbering old Transit van, and once they had passed Lancaster with the dome of the Ashton memorial clearly visible across the fields, it was quieter. Benno relaxed enough to talk to his passenger.

"So, where is this caravan?"

"Near Windemere. It's not far from the town with all the shops and pubs. But we'll keep our heads down for a bit. Nobody'll take any notice of us and we can plan what we do next."

"How do you mean, next?"

"Well, we can't stay there for that long. This bloke rents it out, and it's coming up to summer."

"How do you know there's nobody there now?"

Daz sighed and shifted on the seat, turning to look more directly at Benno. "I don't, do I? But at least I've come up with an idea. You haven't. All you do is moan and whine and complain."

"Yeah, but, Daz, I don't want to do this. I never wanted this to happen. I just thought…"

"Yeah, you thought what?"

"To be honest, I didn't really think anything. When we found that gun, it seemed like a buzz. But it wasn't. I should never have shown it to you. Me and Stick just went along with it because you said. We should have never done it. I wish we hadn't now. Wish we'd never done none of it. I hate this. I want to go home."

To his shame, tears leaked from his eyes, and he sniffed and coughed, but he knew Daz had seen them. The other lad raised the big knife again.

"You need to man up, mate," Daz said. "I'm not kidding. If I get the idea you're gonna drop me in it, you'll be bloody sorry. You're in this as much as me."

"I never hit nobody."

"That won't make any difference to the bizzies. You were there. You're what they call 'an accessory', and they'll lock you up and throw away the key. A dead old woman on the books. They won't care what happened, they'll just want a result."

"We can tell them we didn't mean it…"

"Don't be so bloody stupid. No, mate, forget home. You're not going home ever again. We're going off somewhere else."

"But, Daz, where?"

Daz thumped at the dashboard. "I don't know yet, do I? I need time to think. Once we get to the caravan, I'll plan the next move. Your job is just to drive this wreck and, honest to God, I could do that better myself."

"What about Stick?"

"What about him?"

"They'll have found him, won't they? And they'll get him some help."

"Might have. Might not have done yet."

"Yeah, they will, cos…" It was too late. Benno hoped he'd get away with the slip of the tongue. He held his breath.

Chapter 33

Stella rang to say that the vehicle owner was in the Trauma Unit at the Royal Preston Hospital. He was still hanging on, but she hadn't been able to talk to him. The paramedics had been treating him for the whole of the blue-light journey. She'd since had a word with one of the nurses and asked if they could at least try to get the registration number of his car. Apparently, she was still smarting from the filthy look she was given.

Jordan told her that the ambulance carrying Stick was headed for the same hospital. "He's not too good, but by the time they took him away, they'd decided he wasn't as bad as it had seemed at first," Jordan told her. "His parents have been informed and are on their way."

Jordan and John were viewing the car park CCTV. They had watched the white van arrive and even seen Benno and Daz eating their burgers.

"It's heartless, isn't it?" John said. "The way they just leave their mate in the back of the van and go off."

Jordan nodded, but he was concentrating; watching as poor old Hargreaves hobbled back to his car. He had a plastic carrier in one hand and struggled with it and his stick as he tried to dig his car keys out of his jacket pocket.

Daz had waited until he was fumbling with the shopping and the car door and then came up behind him, the big knife held discreetly by his side. He glanced around and once he had confirmed that the coast was clear, he wrapped an arm around the old man's neck, the blade against his throat.

It was hard to watch. They could see the panic as Hargreaves dropped his shopping and his stick clattered to the floor. Daz spun him around and they glimpsed his terrified face before he was pushed roughly to the ground and rolled towards the scrappy bushes at the edge of the car park. Daz was kneeling beside him, leaning forward and hissing into his face. They couldn't hear what was said, but the old man had raised shaking hands to protect himself.

Benno appeared, hefting a holdall. He bent to retrieve the keys from where they had fallen. He slid into the driving seat, throwing the bag into the rear and then, with a final kick at the prostrate pensioner, Daz had jumped into the car, and they had sped away.

"Jesus, that's horrible," John said.

Jordan found he couldn't speak. He had found the vicious cruelty too terrible.

"We need to have a word with the security people. Why did nobody spot what was going on? The CCTV is supposed to be monitored," John said.

"Yep. We'll put it in the report, but it's too late now, so we just need to work with what we've got," Jordan said.

They had the make and model and colour of the car and the number would already be recorded by the ANPR system. If it was on the major roads, it was only a matter of time before it would be picked up.

Jordan saw a message from Kath drop into his inbox. A quick glance showed him it was the report on the gun that had been found in the back of the Mercedes. It wasn't important right then, and he clicked the phone closed again as they went back to his Golf, so they were ready to go when the old man's Ford Focus was spotted.

Chapter 34

It was fully dark now and raining. The lorries thundering past were rocking the smaller car and Benno was quiet. Leaning forward and peering through the rain-swept windscreen, now and then he would hiss through his teeth.

"How much further on this bloody motorway?" he said.

"Not far. It's just up here. Take the A590 at junction 36. Then we have to watch for the signs."

"Well, you're gonna have to watch out. I'm busy, like, just watching the road."

"It's not for a bit yet. I'll tell you." Daz gazed out of the window at the hedges and fields with the odd farmhouse lights beaming through the dark. Suddenly, he sat up.

"There– there, that roundabout, the sign that says 'Crook'."

"What?"

"We need to head for a place called Crook. We go past the Sun Inn pub, we always used to stop there. This is brilliant, this is."

Daz was behaving as if he was on holiday. Benno just wanted it all to be over.

Once away from the main road, visibility was reduced even further.

"I can't see nothing," Benno said. "It's dark. They must have had a power cut or something. There's nothing."

"Have you never been here? You've never been to the Lakes?"

"No, why would anyone come here? There's nothing."

"Where did you go for your holidays?"

"We went to proper places. We always went to Spain or Majorca."

"Well, we came here and stayed in the caravan. I used to like it here, with my dad and the boat."

Daz directed them down winding roads which became darker and narrower. Trees blew and shook in a growing wind, and leaves and detritus skidded across the tarmac. Streaks of silver rain filled the cone of light from the full beam headlights, making it yet more difficult to see. It was quiet save for the sing of the wet road under the wheels, the purr of the engine, and Benno's heavy breathing. There were no other cars in the inhospitable darkness. When a low, dark shape scuttled across the road, Benno swerved wildly, colliding with the bank, sending sods of grass flying and stalling the engine.

"Oh shit, oh shit!" he said. "What the hell was that?" He lay his head on the steering wheel, his hands covering his eyes.

Once it was clear that they were safe, Daz began to laugh, a genuinely amused sound, which was unusual for him. Normally, his hilarity was forced and cynical, but now he was just laughing.

Benno raised his head and stared across the car. "What the hell are you laughing at?"

"Your face, you wuss. You should see yourself."

"Yeah, but there was a bear."

This made Daz laugh louder. The tension of the last hours exploded in hysteria. After a few minutes, Benno reversed onto the carriageway and pulled onto the verge.

"Shut the fuck up," Benno said. "Just stop it, right? Just don't laugh at me. What was that? Bloody bears and God knows what else, and you're sitting there laughing like some daft bird."

"It wasn't no bear, you plonker. It was a badger. Just a lickle weenie badger and Benno was frightened." Daz laughed again.

Benno threw open the car door and pushed himself out into the rain.

Daz leaned across. "What you doing? Get back in, it's freezing. Yous is letting the rain in."

"No." Benno snorted through his nose and turned back and forth, shaking his head. "No, that's enough. I'm not doing this no more. I didn't want to be here. I'm not going off with you. I want to go home. This place is bloody horrible. I hate that you hit the old woman, then that old bloke, and we're in his car. I hate we left Stick, and he might even be dead, and I hate you, Daz. I really do."

He knew as he said it, he should have kept his mouth shut. It was shock and sadness and despair, and he knew it could end in disaster.

Benno didn't know what to do. His hair was plastered to his head by the downpour and his shoulders were soaked, the hoody sagging with water.

Daz wasn't laughing now. He slid across the seat and out of the driver's door. The blade glinted in the glow from the interior light as he raised it in front of him. He twisted it back and forth in his hand.

Benno backed off, holding up his hands. "Stop it, Daz. Just stop it, right?"

Daz stepped closer. He bent forward, his arm outstretched, the knife weaving from side to side.

"You can't drive. If you hurt me, what you gonna do?" Benno whispered. "How are you going to get to this precious caravan without me?"

Out of the darkness came the bright beam of headlights as a car swept around the corner. The big SUV slowed as it approached and crept forward. Daz had the knife by his side and Benno dragged his dripping hood over his head.

They moved to the side of the road to let the chunky vehicle pass, but it slowed and stopped. The window lowered with a quiet shush.

"You got a problem?" The driver, a middle-aged man, glanced back and forth, peering at the parked car. "You got a flat or something?"

"No, it's nothing. My mate just freaked when we saw a badger," Daz laughed. "He's okay now, though. Thanks."

"Where are you off to? It's late, a foul night as well."

Benno held his breath. He knew that Daz didn't take kindly to being questioned, ever. He couldn't cope with yet more violence.

Daz stepped closer to the big car. "We're going to my mate's caravan, but we got held up earlier. It's over near Windemere, but it's sound now. Thanks, though," he said.

"Okay, well, take care, lads."

And it was over. The tail lights faded into the distance and the heat had gone from the moment.

"Come on, soft lad. Get back in the car. We'll get some chips first place we see and a couple of cans for when we get to the caravan."

There was no real choice, and Benno slouched back to the car and pulled away, heading into the darkness.

Chapter 35

There was nothing more to be gained by staying at the services. The white van was cordoned off with police tape and once the SOCO team gave the all-clear, the vehicle would be taken back to Liverpool on the back of a trailer.

Jordan headed off to Preston hospital where Hargreaves and Stick were in the Major Trauma Unit and only allowed to have family visits – Stick's mum and dad were on the way but the old man had no one. Stella had searched his pockets, so they had an address. A uniformed officer called at the small, terraced house in Preston, and found it in darkness. Neighbours confirmed that the old man lived alone and had one brother who lived 'somewhere down south'.

"Once they're off the motorway, it's going to be a lot harder to spot them," John said. "They'll be pretty much out in the wilds if they take the minor roads. I wonder if there's any point asking for the chopper?"

Jordan shook his head. "We haven't a clue where to send them. Our best hope is the troops on the ground and the traffic cameras."

It was frustrating, but there was very little more they could do. They knew who had injured the old man and Stick. They knew who had carried out the vicious attacks in the post office. There was no mystery here, and yet still they didn't have them.

The temptation to get into the car and drive up the motorway was huge, but they knew it was pointless. Waiting for the possibility of a chance with Stick was the only thing they could think to do. One more car going in the same direction as all the others was a waste of resources.

Jordan went in search of coffee and chocolate biscuits. Struggling back through the door into the unit, he met John coming the other way.

"They've been seen. Check your messages."

All three had their phones on vibrate and Jordan carrying the cups and the sweets hadn't been able to pull his from his pocket.

"What, tell me?" he said as they stormed through the quiet corridors, Jordan still juggling the cardboard cup holder.

"Response to the alert on the Cumbrian Police website. There's a bloke, a magistrate, spends a happy hour with his single malt before bed, perusing the police sites. Thank God for weird old farts. Anyway, he saw two young lads in a grey Focus at the side of the road to Crook. They said they were heading for a caravan in Windermere. He's convinced it was Daz and Benno. Stella's outside on Airwave getting things moving. Trouble is, it was about an hour ago that he saw them. Could be they'll be in Windemere by now."

"Are there many caravans around there?" Jordan asked. John's raised eyebrows told him all he needed to know.

It was going to be a long night. He called Penny to let her know he probably wouldn't be home before morning. He asked if she'd call Pete at the Titanic Hotel and let him know the weekend was probably a non-starter. She promised to do it first thing on Saturday. She told him to take care, and that she loved him.

"I need someone at Daz's parents' house and Benno's immediately, to find out where his uncle has got to. Get them out of bed if necessary. If these two are heading for a caravan in Windemere, it must be somewhere they already know. It's just not the sort of place a couple of yobs like these would choose. London and a hotel, maybe even the streets, if they had to, but a caravan in the Lake District — there has to be a reason," Jordan said.

Chapter 36

The rain had eased and the lights gleaming on the roads and pavements in Bowness settled Benno's jangled nerves. They couldn't see much of the shops and houses, and Daz gave wrong directions a couple of times, but when he saw the road he recognised, he leaned forward, pointing through the windscreen, perching on the edge of the seat. Benno had never seen him so animated.

They left the town and out in the country the darkness deepened. Thick stands of trees tunnelled parts of the road.

"How much further?" Benno asked.

"It's here somewhere," Daz said. "There's a farm. It's got a road leading to it and the caravans are at the back."

A couple of minutes later, he jigged excitedly on the seat. "There. It's there. That's the gate."

A wooden five-bar gate leaned drunkenly from its hinges.

Daz peered into the gloom. "I can't see the house. It's late though. They used to have lights outside. I suppose they can't afford the leccy anymore."

Benno turned the car into the potholed drive. A square stone house squatted beside a barn with a collapsed roof. As they neared, they saw that the windows in the main building were boarded up, and weeds grew in the gutters and round the front door.

"This can't be right, mate," Benno said.

"Yeah, yeah it is. I recognise it for sure. It's deserted. They've gone. I don't believe it."

"What we gonna do?" Benno said.

"Wait, just wait. The caravan might still be there. Stay here while I look."

Using the torch on the old man's phone, he splashed across the farmyard and Benno saw the sweep of light on the cliff behind the buildings.

It wasn't long before Daz jogged back. He pulled open the door and gave a thumbs up. "It's still here. There's two of them and they're still here. It's okay. Leave the car by the house. It's too wet round there and then bring the bag and the scran. Don't forget the cans. Come on, it's okay."

"But give us a hand, I can't carry everything," Benno said.

With a sigh, Daz stood and waited as Benno pulled the car in front of the tumbledown barn and clambered out. He was tired and scared, and desperately unhappy. There was nothing he could think of to do but follow Daz back to where two caravans crouched under a steep cliff facing a field, with the lake a black mirror in the distance.

"What's up there?" he asked, pointing at the hillside.

"It's just a field at the top, but you can get back to the main road that way. It's dead steep but I've done it a coupla times. There's a brilliant view."

Benno wasn't impressed with the idea of a steep climb, even for a brilliant view. He shrugged and reached into the carrier to take out a bag of crisps.

Daz stretched full length in the wet earth, scrabbling under the end of the caravan, his fingers running along the edge of the chassis. When he pulled out his hand holding a small box, his teeth glinted in the darkness. "Still in the same place. Belter." He slid the top open, picked out a set of keys, and waved them in front of Benno.

The caravan was clean, but cold and damp. Daz couldn't remember how to start the generator which stood between the two units.

"I was a kid. I didn't do shit like that."

They pulled the curtains closed and lit the candle that was on the table. The water wasn't turned on, so there was to be no shower, not even a wash. The double bed in the little bedroom had no bedding. In the cupboards, there was a half-empty jar of olives and a couple of tea bags in a tin.

They had cans and food and for a little while, sitting in the candle lights drinking lager and eating chicken and bacon sandwiches, Benno felt his spirits rise.

"So, tomorrow?" he said.

"Yeah. We'll have to keep our heads down. But nobody knows we're here and as long as we don't make any fuss, it'll be ace."

"But what are we doing, then?"

Benno saw the look of impatience on Daz's face and felt his heart jump, but Daz just shrugged and sniffed.

"Dunno yet. Might get up to Scotland. I'd like that, or go to the Island. There's a ferry from Heysham. It's the races in a few weeks. We could make that, and nobody'll look for us there."

Benno had never been to the Isle of Man and again, the sadness of the situation swept over him. Going to the Island with his mates should have been a blast. He'd heard the motorbikes coming back from the TT and the GP, streaming off the boats in Liverpool, roaring up the motorway by the hundreds. He'd always found it thrilling.

Daz slid out from the bench seat. "We don't want to use the bog, not with the water off. I'll go outside and, if you need a shit, you'll just have to go in the bushes. Tomorrow I'll get stuff sorted."

Alone in the dim light, Benno took out his phone and booted it up. He was surprised that there was signal but then Daz had said the road was near the top of the cliff so maybe they weren't as far from civilization as he imagined. The thought was a comfort. He clicked on his text messages. There were seven from his dad. They became increasingly frantic and there were four voice messages pleading with him to let them know where he was and what was happening.

He sighed. This was all so complicated now. The messages told him that the police had been to the house asking if they knew where he might have gone. They were looking for him and all he had to do was let them know he was all right and they would sort it all out. One told him that Stick was really bad and in the hospital but would probably be okay in the end. They didn't mention the old bloke, so he could only hope they hadn't been told about that.

He clicked open the messaging app.

I'm OK. Gotta keep low 4 now don't worry

He clicked send as Daz slid back into his seat. "Whatcha doin'?" He reached out and snatched the phone.

"You pillock. You moron. Aw shit, Benno. What did I say?"

He pulled back his hand and flung the phone the length of the caravan. It slammed into the wall and fell to the floor in pieces. Benno jumped up, but Daz was quicker and, raising his foot high, he stamped over and over on the broken device.

Benno kneeled on the floor, scraping all the tiny pieces together and this time when the tears flowed across his face, he let them drip from his chin as he stared at the broken plastic in his hand.

Daz was cursing and stuffing things back into his bag. He kicked out at the wall. He turned to look at Benno standing in the middle of the little living room, his head lowered.

"I've had it with you. You're a bloody div."

"But where are you going, Daz? I'm sorry, like. I didn't think but my mam and dad won't dob me in."

"They won't need to. The pigs'll be tracing your phone. It's dead easy for them now."

"But you broke it, didn't you? They won't be able to find it smashed to pieces."

"Of course they will. I've seen it. They use triangles or something with the masts."

"It's triangulation, but they probably won't be able to out here in the back of beyond. I don't reckon so. Anyway, where are you going?"

"Anywhere away from you."

"It's the middle of the night. Just wait till morning. They won't be looking for us in the middle of the night. Then I'll drive you anywhere. The train, the bus. Or maybe we can go up to Scotland like you said. Only, Daz, don't leave me on my own. I'm sorry, I know I'm a wuss and that, but I can't stay here, it's the middle of nowhere and there's – whatchamacallits – badgers and stuff. You know what to do, please, mate. I'm scared."

Daz looked on with barely disguised disgust as Benno wiped tears from his face. He blew out his cheeks and then threw himself onto the long seat.

Chapter 37

They didn't wait any longer than absolutely necessary. Once the relief had arrived to stand guard at the hospital, Jordan, Stella, and John piled into the Golf and headed up the motorway. They would be informed if Stick became able to talk. Cumbria Police had asked if they needed an escort, but the offer was half-hearted and accompanied by the comment that they were short-staffed, and it could be a while before anyone would be available. Jordan had told them they were only information gathering and although everyone knew that wasn't true, it cleared the decks for them to head off on their own.

The sky had cleared, and the moonlight streaked the trees and grass verges with silver, glinting on puddles and small ponds. There was little traffic, and they made good time to the turn-off for Crook.

When the call came from Liverpool with the location of the caravan, John let out a yell and thumped the back of the seat.

"Let's get the little sods," he said.

"Don't get too excited," Stella said. "We aren't sure they're there. This is just where Daz's mother remembers them going for holidays when he was little. What are the chances that he'd remember?"

"I don't think Daz has that many happy memories, so maybe this will have stuck. Let's hope so," Jordan said.

"You sound as though you're sorry for him, boss," Stella said.

"I wouldn't say that. What he's done is nasty and vicious, but something made him that way. His life is ruined and now we just have to catch him before he does any more harm. Don't forget, Benno is with him and we don't know yet who did what. My betting is that it's Daz who's the ringleader, though. Benno is the driver with his provisional licence, so it makes sense he was in the car outside during the robberies. It could have been Stick who struck the blow in the post office, but from the witness statements, it wasn't the skinny one. That leaves us Daz, and we know for certain it was him that hit Hargreaves; we saw it." Jordan shrugged. "He's going away for a long time and even though he'll still be young when he comes out, what is he going to do with his life, with this in the background?"

They drove through Bowness, sleeping and deserted, apart from a couple of prowling cats and the sound of an owl calling to the night.

They stopped before the turn for the farm and climbed out, shocked by the chill after the warmth in the car.

Daz's mother had been cold and monosyllabic when the uniformed officer tried to question her, but she had given them a rough idea of where the caravan was. She made the point that it was years since she'd been there. She didn't have contact details for her former partner's mate, who owned the caravan, and in her opinion, it was stupid to think her son had gone back there.

"He's not into that stuff anymore," she had said. "He wants to shoot at things on the internet and play those stupid racing games. Why would he want to go out there when there's nothing but trees and hills and water and bloody rain? All the time, rain."

Jordan led the way along the muddy drive towards the deserted buildings. "Over there," Stella said. "That's Hargreaves's car."

Jordan held up his hand for them to stop at the corner of the house and pointed to the two green-painted units. They could see no sign of life.

Chapter 38

Daz had claimed the bedroom, stretching out fully clothed, with his dirty shoes, smearing the mattress. Benno pulled out the folding bed from the seating area. He slipped off his trainers and pulled a rug from the back of a chair. Curled into a foetal ball, he tried to shut everything out. He shivered, partly from the chill and partly from fear of what the next day might hold.

After a while, he gave up the struggle for sleep and swung his legs round to sit on the edge of the thin cushions. It was the middle of the night and pitch dark. He had no phone for a torch. The candle had burned out long ago and the only relief was the glint of the moon as it sneaked through a gap in the curtains and reflected from a glass cupboard door. He rolled across the bed and kneeled to peer through into the dark yard and the cliff rising behind it.

The movement at the corner of his vision made his heart jump and stopped his breathing. He pushed his face closer to the glass, rubbed at the condensation with his sleeve and squinted into the gloom. The stunted trees near the old barn shivered in the wind and where the grass had grown long over the winter, there was a rustling. He squeezed his eyes closed for a moment, shook his shoulders. He had to get it together or Daz would leave him behind.

He heard a crunch on the loose gravel path. There was no mistake now. Clearly footsteps, and this was no cat or badger.

He ran through to the bedroom and shook Daz awake.

"What the hell, Benno?" Daz pushed Benno's arms away and struggled to a sitting position.

"There's someone outside, Daz. For sure. I saw a shadow, then I heard someone walking on the gravel."

Daz was fully awake now, swinging his feet to the floor and rubbing at his eyes. "You sure?"

"For certain, mate. Coming from the yard."

"It was all empty."

"I know. That's why I woke you. There's something going on."

They crawled across the narrow room and kneeled below the window. Daz lifted the edge of the flowered curtain, and they peered outside. The dark figures of Stella and John were standing beside the back wall of the house and as they watched, Jordan joined them and pointed towards the caravan.

"Shit, shit it's the bizzies," Daz said. "It must be. This is your fault. You and the fucking phone. Grab the bag, Benno. We need to get out the back."

"There's no door, mate. The door's at the side, they'll see us."

"I know, shithead. We're going out the window. We're going now."

As he spoke, Daz crawled across the mattress and wrestled for a minute with the catch. Once he had pushed the window open, he turned back to where Benno stood holding the sports bag. He reached and grabbed it, then turned to push it out into the narrow strip of land between the unit and the cliff.

With his legs kicking and pushing, Daz squirmed his body through and out. Benno heard him land with a thud. He looked at the narrow space, and then down at his body. He could see immediately that it was going to be a squeeze. There was no choice. He dragged off his bulky hoody and pushed it out ahead of him, then reached with his arms, pushed his shoulders into the gap and felt the frame grip his body.

"I don't think I can fit through," he hissed.

Daz grabbed his hands and tugged him forward. "Come on, you wuss. Try."

Benno tried, he really tried very hard, but his body was too big for the space. It was useless and as Daz dropped his hands and turned to pick up the bag of money, he knew he was left behind and it was over.

Daz turned and jabbed a finger towards the window. "Don't you dob me in, shithead. You do and I'll come for you," he hissed.

As Benno pushed back into the room, he saw his friend jog on the rough ground and sling the bag across his shoulder as he prepared to scale the rocks at the back of the site. He saw the light from a torch flash in the room and heard the door rattle. There was no point in doing anything other than giving up and letting it all happen. He walked through to the living room, pulled the woollen throw from the settee to wrap around his shoulders, and went to the seating area to fasten his shoelaces.

Chapter 39

There were footprints in the wet soil. It looked very much as though someone had accessed the caravan.

Jordan rattled the door and knocked with the side of his fist. "Police, come on, lads. Give it up now. We know you're in there."

There was no response, and he thumped on the aluminium panel again and jiggled the handle up and down. There still no response, and Stella jogged around to the back of the unit. She called out as she spotted Daz scrambling up the steep rocks at the base of the cliff.

"Police. Stand still. You can't get away, you pillock, just keep still."

Jordan and John ran to join her, and Jordan launched himself up over the boulders to where the cliff rose steeply above them. Daz had already begun to climb. Small rocks and soil showered down around where Jordan was looking for a handhold.

"Hang on, boss," Stella shouted. "It's not safe, that's too steep."

Jordan found a tiny ledge for his toes and reached with his hands, looking for a place for his fingertips. His shoes were slick leather, and he had no gloves. He quickly realised he wasn't going to get very far, so jumped back and tilted his head to look up. Daz was making progress in his flexible trainers, with more to lose and fewer years under his belt. He was already over fifteen metres up the face of the cliff. As he struggled with the steepening side, the bag with the strap over one shoulder pulled and swung, dragging at his body each time he moved.

The window behind them opened and Benno leaned out. "Daz, mate, come back down. They've got us. Just give it up."

John turned and pointed at the boy. "You get that bloody door open right now."

He stormed back to where Benno was unlocking the front door. He stomped into the van and grabbed the boy, dragged his hands behind him, locking on the speed cuffs. He pushed him onto the settee.

"Stay there and shut up." He snarled. "I'll be back for you."

He took the key from the lock, slammed the door closed and locked it behind him. Back at the rear, Jordan and Stella were watching Daz, moving slowing now, struggling against the steep cliff and the pull of the bag on his shoulder. He had glanced down at them once but ignored their shouts and pleas to just stop and come back.

His foot slipped on the slick rocks and swung out into midair. They heard him cry and Jordan ran again to the foot of the cliff. He knew that trying to climb was only going to make matters worse, but the helplessness was torment.

"Daz, come on, lad. Come down slowly. We'll help you. This can all be sorted if you just come back with us now. There's nowhere else for you to go."

Daz twisted his neck to peer down at them. The bag shifted on his shoulder, and they heard him groan. He moved his feet and found a wider ledge and for a moment, it seemed he would recover. He stretched up with his arms, fingers reaching, and grabbed onto a shrub growing from a crack in the rock.

"Don't, Daz. Don't use that. It'll never hold you," Jordan shouted.

They watched in despair as he wrapped his hand tightly around the trunk of the little bush and they saw his arms and shoulders tense as he bent his knee to lift his foot higher. The jutting rock he was aiming for shifted and fell. He gave a short, terrified cry. The shrub pulled from the cleft and Stella gasped 'no' as they watched him lose all hold on the cliff. It was probably over in seconds, but it seemed like an age as time slowed and the three detectives ran forwards to try to save the falling boy.

Chapter 40

Benno pleaded with John to let him go to where his friend lay broken and bloody among the wet boulders at the foot of the cliff. He was told there was nothing he could do. Nothing anyone could do. Still, he sobbed.

"Maybe you're wrong," he said. "You're not a doctor. You could be wrong. Let me see."

They had taken off the handcuffs and wrapped a survival blanket from the first aid kit in Jordan's car around his shoulders, but the boy had rigors.

John shook his head. "It's not happening, lad. Apart from anything else, there'd be hell to pay if we let you."

They let Benno speak to his mum on John's phone. It was hard to watch as he sobbed and told her he hadn't meant any of it to happen and begged her to help him.

Jordan wanted to go personally to Daz's mum's house but it would be a long time before they were back in Liverpool and by then the media would have the story and it just wasn't fair to let her find out that way. A family liaison officer and a uniformed sergeant had the unhappy task.

Back in the Lakes, an ambulance had collected Daz's body. It would have been more correct to call the medical examiner, but it was quicker to have the body taken to the hospital rather than wait for the team to come from Cockermouth. With three witnesses to the fall, there wasn't going to be much doubt as to what had cut this young life short. When the paramedics arrived, Stella was still administering CPR. She knew it was hopeless, but that wasn't her call to make. They didn't want to leave him in the rain with his jacket covering his face, so they agreed they'd take the flak if there was any, and the paramedics were happy to go along with them.

It would be a cross-force case. The assault on Hargreaves and the theft of his car were separate from the robberies and death in Liverpool, which meant more paperwork than normal, and Jordan arranged to come back with Stella to the Cumbrian headquarters during the following week. First, they all needed some rest. Once the scene had been handed over and Benno was sent off in prisoner transport to the cells in Copy Lane, Jordan, Stella, and John piled into the car to head back home with a stop on the motorway for sandwiches and coffee.

It was a quiet journey. They had solved the case but at huge cost and none of them felt it was a success.

"I'm going to get Benno checked in and then home for a few hours," Jordan said. "In the morning, I'll go to the station to start the reports and do the interview. I reckon he'll get bail. He's not going anywhere, he's in bits. I'll speak to the hospital. Then I'm taking the afternoon off. You guys have the weekend, and we'll get back to it all on Monday."

* * *

Back in Crosby, Jordan's wife had hot chocolate waiting for him and the electric blanket warming his bed.

Harry was asleep; they sat in the quiet of early morning and Penny let him relax.

"I'm going in for a couple of hours in the morning and then we'll go for lunch instead of dinner, if you like," he said. "Then the great bed shop."

"There was no answer when I tried to get in touch with Peter. I've tried a couple of times," Penny said.

"Not to worry. What we can do is go to the hotel and see what the situation is. If he can't make it for any reason, we'll treat ourselves while we're there. It's odd that he hasn't been in touch, though."

Chapter 41

Jordan was surprised to hear the voice of DCI Josh Lewis on the desk phone calling him up to the office. It was unusual for him to be working on a Saturday morning and with no secretarial support.

He had hoped to achieve all he had planned in just a couple of hours and the clock was already ticking on the time that Benno had been held. There was no way around it, though. When the boss called, you had to answer.

The opening salvo was harsh. "I'll need a full report about yesterday and the injured and the dead. This has turned into a bit of a debacle, Detective Inspector."

"Not the result we would have hoped for, sir," Jordan said. "But I don't know that we could have done anything different. We found the suspects as quickly as we could. The harm to the old man and the one they called Stick had already happened. I sincerely wish that we could have avoided what happened to Daniel, but he was scared and running; there was no way we could have reached him in time. We did try, but he landed on the rocks. They'll be doing a post-mortem exam at the beginning of next week, but we already know what killed him, unfortunately."

"How are the two in hospital?"

"I phoned on my way in, sir. Stick, that's Simon Brown, is recovering and under caution in the hospital, and we'll interview him on Monday. The old man, Mr Hargreaves, has been moved from into the cardiology department and is doing well. We've got a statement, but there is CCTV of the attack on him as well, so there's no mystery there. I'm going now to interview Benno, that's, Benjamin Midgely. His uncle is coming in as the responsible adult. He might be here now."

"Okay, keep me informed."

Jordan turned to leave.

"Just one more thing, DI Carr," said Lewis.

"Sir?"

"Apparently there was a report from the Met about the gun that was used in the post office robberies. I've had a complaint that there has been no response at all regarding that. They are in the middle of a major investigation down there and expected more assistance from us. They pointed out that they rushed a report to us to try to help out."

"I haven't had a chance to read the full report yet, sir. It came in when I was in the middle of trying to find the lads."

"Well, make time now, yes? They want information as soon as possible."

"I'll know more when I've spoken to Benno. Actually, I wouldn't have been able to tell them very much before now."

"Hmm, get a shift on, would you? Make sure that's done before you leave today. I don't expect complaints like this about my senior officers."

It was unfair, but there was no point arguing the toss. Once he talked to Benno, he would be able to send something off to London. Jordan glanced at his watch. The day was getting away from him already and he knew Penny was looking forward to the lunch out instead of the evening that had originally been planned. He would hate to disappoint her again.

As he walked down the corridor, he spotted Stella turning into the main incident room. "I told you to have the weekend off, Stel."

"Yeah, but I thought I could help out here, and it's my brother's kid's birthday… I'd been roped in to help at the party and this was far more appealing. Work is the only excuse that they can't argue against."

"Do me a favour then, will you?"

"Anything, boss."

"Go through the report about the gun and see if there's anything specific I need to know while I'm in with Benno. I'll find out how they came to have it and what have you, but if there's anything else, just let me know."

"On it, boss."

* * *

Benno was bedraggled and red eyed when they brought him into the interview room. His hair was greasy and lank. The tracksuit he had been given to wear stretched tight across his belly and his trainers, without the laces, slapped and dragged as he walked.

"Are you okay?" Jordan asked.

"No."

"Is there anything you need?"

"I need to go home. I need Daz to have not fallen and all of this not to have happened."

As Benno dissolved in tears, Frank reached out to lay a hand on his shoulder.

"Come on, lad. I know this is horrible, but you have to pull yourself together. Man up and answer the questions. Then we might be able to get off home."

The older man looked across the table at Jordan, who could only shrug.

"The best thing you can do now, Benjamin, is to tell me everything you know," said Jordan. "Then we'll see what we can do. You'll feel better when it's all off your chest, anyway. Let's start with the gun. Where did that come from? If you bought it, I need to know who sold it to you. You know that's illegal. You're not stupid."

Chapter 42

A uniformed officer was sitting in on the interview. Stella or John would have been first choice, but John wasn't there, and Jordan hoped that by giving his sergeant the gun report to read, he could cut down on the time it all took.

Benno was nervous and trying to avoid saying anything that he thought would make matters worse. After the first outburst, he slouched on the chair, his arms crossed, and legs stretched under the table. Every question was met with a shake of his head, a shrug, or a sullen 'dunno'. It was getting them nowhere.

"If this is all you're going to say, then we might as well just send you back to the cell until you're ready to talk to us," Jordan said.

It was maddening. There was probably not enough to apply for an extension and the clock was ticking down to when they had to let him go. So, they would have to charge him as an accessory to the robberies and the beating of Hargreaves. The chances were that once they did that, the uncle would ask for legal representation and everything would grind to a halt. A clever lawyer could probably show that all the evidence against Benno was circumstantial or that he had been under threat from Daz and in fear for his safety.

Stick had already said that he was going to plead guilty to everything and just wanted it over. It was ironic that of the three youths, he was probably the one who might have had a decent future. He wasn't the murderer; like Benno, he was an also-ran.

It was very possible that Benno would walk away. There were witnesses from inside the shop, but no one had given them a description of the car driver apart from it being a fat lad with a ski mask on.

"I don't want to go back to that cell. If I tell you what you want to know, can I go home?" Benno said.

There was nothing to gain from obfuscation. "I can't promise you that," Jordan told him. "There's no getting around it. You're in big trouble. If you help us, it will help you, but you must know that what you've been involved in is serious."

"But I didn't do nothing. I didn't hit that old woman, or the old bloke neither. It wasn't me that hit Stick. I wouldn't do that. Jesus, I would never do that. He's a mate." Benno was overwhelmed now and tears kept running down his cheeks. Jordan took a pack of tissues from his pocket and handed them over.

"So, who did?" Jordan said, as Benno blew his nose, hard, and then screwed the tissue in his hands, bits falling onto his lap as he picked and tore at it.

"I s'pose now he's dead it can't do him no harm. It was Daz. He had the gun in the post office, and he just got narked with Stick at the allotment. I don't reckon he meant to really hurt him."

"And Stick?"

"No, he never hit nobody. He was there, but he didn't know that was going to happen and he was proper gutted."

"So, where did the gun come from?"

Benno looked across at Frank. "Do I have to say?"

Frank sighed. "Oh, just get on with it. This isn't serving any purpose. Tell him" – he pointed at Jordan – "what you did."

"I found it. When I went out in the van collecting stuff; it was in a skip. I didn't even know it was real. I thought it was a fake. Even after I got it, I pulled the trigger and stuff, and nothing happened."

"You stupid sod," Frank said, throwing his hands in the air. "I can't believe what an absolute div you are. You could have killed somebody." As he realised what he had said, his face flushed, and he shook his head and groaned. "I didn't mean that he would," he said to Jordan.

"Okay," Jordan said. "So, whose idea was it to use it for the robberies?"

"It was Daz. It started as a joke, at least I thought it was, but then he just went on and before we knew what was happening, we were all in it with him. He wanted money to leave home proper, like, and set up somewhere else."

Once he had begun, Benno laid it all out for them, and there were no real surprises.

"So, this skip?" Jordan asked. "Where was it?"

"Crosby." Benno turned to his uncle. "D'ya remember that pile of stuff from the big house makeover? It was there in the garden, and I just looked in on the off chance there was something worth having."

"I need an address," Jordan said.

"I dunno, do I? It was one of them posh houses with the big gardens. It was down by that school. The private one."

Jordan's phone vibrated on the table with a message from Stella.

> *Gun used in a homicide in London. Suspect on the lam. They're asking for help to search for him here, now.*

"Benno," Jordan said. "You are deep in the shit. You can help yourself, though. It's up to you. If you play ball with us now, things will move more quickly. You might get bail. Not up to me, but I'll let them know if you co-operate. I need your written statement about the gun and exactly where found it. Exactly where, when, and how. Somebody will come in to do that with you."

The youth's eyes lit up with the idea of release, and he nodded enthusiastically.

Back in his office, Jordan brought the ballistic report up on his screen. He intended to send a quick email back to the Met with the information they had and to promise he'd look into it further. Then, he saw the names.

Chapter 43

Stella was typing out her report when Jordan went back to the incident room. He walked through, raised a hand in greeting, and carried on to his own office.

She waited for a while, and then, taking him a mug of coffee, she knocked on the door. "Everything okay, boss?"

He glanced up from the screen and frowned at her. "What? Oh, yes, sure, everything's fine."

"You got the precis of the report from London then. Don't see that it'll make much difference to our case, and I don't think we know much to tell them. I mean, did Benno tell you where he got the gun?"

Jordan repeated what the lad had said about finding the weapon.

She shrugged. "Well, that might be of some help, but we already knew it had been in the rubbish somewhere. I suppose it's confirmation. The chances of SOCO being able to find much, even if he had given you the address, seem pretty slight. There might well be CCTV round there though, with that private school and what have you. Maybe the Met will want to send someone up, but if we can help them avoid that, it's brownie points. So, first thing, we'll have to see if there are any images of this bloke they're looking for. I can see why they got a bit miffed when we didn't get back to them, but we had a lot on. Still, we're on it now." She began to list the things they'd need to do in the suspect's search. "I can get on that if you like. Kath and Vi can start trying to get any CCTV there might be, first thing on Monday. I'll get on to the press office and we can put notices on the websites and in the paper. I don't expect we'll be able to stretch to a house-to-house, but certainly we need to go to the place that was having the work done if we can find it."

"Actually," said Jordan, "I think I'll organise that. Thanks, though."

Stella stared at him for a long minute, frowning. It was basic stuff and not even their own case. She shrugged and walked back to her desk. Jordan could tell she was puzzled, but he needed time to think about this. There were several issues. His mind was whirling, and he needed a few minutes to himself. He closed the office door, which was unusual enough to cause Stella to glance up. After a while, he watched as she gathered her things together, turned her computer off, put her notes away and, without stopping to say goodbye, left the office. He knew she was offended. There had been no reason for handling the simple work himself.

Penny rang to say that she was ready. He arranged to meet her in town. The pleasure was marred now, but he wouldn't disappoint her. They would buy the bed for their son, and then go for lunch. He would suggest somewhere else to eat. Maybe Liverpool One or down by the Albert Dock so that Harry could see the boats.

He should do something. There would be repercussions if it went on for too long. He read the report again, switched off his computer and went to meet his family.

Jordan called ahead to arrange to park at St Anne Street Police Station. Penny travelled from Crosby on the train and when he met them outside Central Station in Ranelagh Street, which was busy with Saturday shoppers and sightseers. Harry was still buzzing with excitement about this new experience.

Penny had done the research. The bed she had chosen was in store and it didn't take them long to decide it was perfect and arrange for delivery.

"Do you want to go to the hotel?" Penny asked.

"Let's just get something by ourselves," Jordan said. "I'm a bit whacked, to be honest, and not up to socializing."

"Are you okay?" Penny said.

He reassured her and they walked the short distance to the pizza restaurant and then, because they hated to disappoint him, and he had come to expect it when they were in the city, they took Harry on the ferry, travelling both ways without disembarking. The wind was chilly, but it was sunny and bright. Gulls whirled over the churning wake and in the distance, a cruise ship sailed majestically away from the Mersey. For just a little while, Jordan let go of the problem and enjoyed the trip.

Harry was sleepy and cranky by the time they were back in the city, and Jordan insisted Penny take the car. He told her he had a couple of things he needed to do. She left him at the main police station and probably assumed that was where he was headed. He stood in the car park to wave her off before he turned and set out on the half-hour walk to the Titanic Hotel.

Chapter 44

Normally, Jordan would have his warrant card in his hand as he approached the hotel reception. He would show it discreetly to the staff. Now, he'd left it in his pocket. The woman at the desk was busy with a check-in and so he stood back and gazed around the entrance hall. There was a glimpse of the water of Stanley Dock through the windows and all around him the famous ship and the White Star Line were commemorated. Pete had been right when he said it was a high-class hotel. The company must really rate Pete to pay for him to stay here.

Of course, once he was able to speak to the receptionist, she told him she wasn't able to deny or confirm whether Mr Roper was a guest. With a sigh, Jordan pulled out his identification.

The receptionist glanced at her colleague for help, but the young man at the other end of the counter was busy on the phone. She blew out her cheeks and then, with a little shuffle of her shoulders, she turned to the keyboard. She frowned at the screen and clicked another couple of keys.

"Could you spell his name for me again?" she said.

Jordan obliged, though it was simple enough. She asked the date of check-in, and Jordan realised he didn't know precisely. He gave her an estimate of the time he had first been told Pete had tried to make contact.

She slowly shook her head. "I'm sorry, he's just not here. He is certainly not a guest right now and I can't find any record of him previously." She held up a finger. "There is just one thing. What company does he work for? It could be that it's been put in under that. There should still be a record of him, but well…" She smiled. "Stuff isn't always the way it should be, is it?"

Jordan knew Pete had mentioned the company name, but his mind was a blank. "Er, oh, hang on," he said.

The girl looked down at the desk and pursed her lips. She waited, glancing at her desk mate who was now watching the back and forth. She looked up again and raised her eyebrows. "This man is your friend?" she said.

"Yes, of course he is. I haven't seen him for a while. I was going to meet him here today and, in the end, we didn't catch up."

She waited.

Jordan wanted to ring Penny in case she could remember, but that would look very weird. He shook his head.

"All I can tell you then, with the information you have" – she smiled, but it didn't disguise the smugness – "is that the person you're looking for doesn't seem to have been a guest. Sorry. Is there anything else I can help you with today?"

"Nope, it's fine."

Jordan turned and glanced around again. He strolled slowly across the hall, stopped to read the dinner menu, and picked up a couple of vouchers from a rack by the door. He turned and smiled at the receptionists, raising a hand in farewell. They stared at him from their places behind the desk. The woman turned to whisper something to her colleague, who shrugged and watched Jordan as he left.

135

There was nothing else for him to do in the city, and he would need to contact the force in London and speak to whoever was in charge of the case. Surely, there was a mistake. Pete Roper was not an unusual name. He had never said the name of his partner, but that didn't mean anything. It was clear the split had been painful. It was quite a coincidence, but surely that was all. No matter how hard he tried to convince himself, there was the strong pulse at the back of his brain telling him that his old friend was possibly in deep trouble and now Jordan would have to act. There wasn't much time before this would look suspicious. He'd already been slow, and soon it would appear deliberate.

Chapter 45

There was a train about to leave Central Station just as Jordan arrived, and he dashed down the stairs and onto the platform. He would need to pay the ticket inspector when he did his round, but that wasn't unusual. The train was busy as always, but he found a quiet corner and rang home.

Penny was in the middle of giving Harry his snack before bed and sounded distracted. He just wanted to let her know he was on his way and that he'd pick up a spit-roast chicken from the takeaway.

"How long will you be?" she said.

"We've just come through Bootle, so about ten minutes to the station."

"Don't do that. I'll order from Uber Eats. You'll be here sooner if you don't have to hang about waiting at the restaurant."

"Are you all right, love?" Jordan said.

"I want you home. I'll explain when you get here. Just come straight home."

His stomach clenched. They had been together a long time, and some things didn't need to be said. She was disturbed and anxious. When the train pulled into Blundellsands and Crosby station, Jordan was already standing by the doors and pushed his way out as they slid apart.

By the time he reached the leafy road of old houses, he was on the verge of breaking into a jog. Instinct saw him scanning the road for loitering figures and cars parked in the shadows. He saw nothing.

His own car was pulled onto the drive with Penny's Mini further in closer to the garage. Everything looked normal. Patches of coloured light spilled out onto the path from the fancy pane in the front door. Illumination glowed from behind the curtains in the little upstairs front room that was Harry's. Jordan stepped onto the narrow concrete walkway in front of the window and peered through the interior shutters, which were closed with the slats still partly open. The lounge was empty, and the table lamps were lit. It looked cosy and welcoming.

He called out as he pushed the door open to let Penny know it was him and that he was home. She wasn't in the kitchen or the dining room. He didn't call out again because Harry was probably asleep. All the lights were on, even in the bathroom.

He eventually found her in the nursery, Harry fast asleep in his cot. She was sitting in the rocking chair and had a woolly shawl around her shoulders. She wasn't reading, even though the night light would have been bright enough, sitting as she was close to where the boy was snuggled down under his blankets. Her mobile phone was on her lap.

As he stepped through the door, she came to meet him and wrapped her arms around his waist and lay her head on his chest. Her body was tense and, as he hugged her, she sighed and then took in a deep breath.

"I wasn't sure what to do and then you rang and said you were on the way. So, I did nothing, but then I thought that might have been a mistake and talked myself into a bit of a state. I really just wanted to make sure Harry was okay."

Jordan checked that the baby monitor was switched on, then took her by the hand and led her downstairs and into the lounge. After he gave her a glass of whisky and poured one for himself, he waited for her to tell him what had happened.

She gave a quick laugh. "I'm probably being a bit too dramatic."

"Not you. Tell me?"

Everything had been fine and normal when she had arrived and pulled into the drive. The alarm was set, and she had disarmed it as they came through the door. She'd sent Harry to play in the dining room and went upstairs.

"I hadn't turned the radio on, but I could hear talking and it was a minute before I realised it was Harry. I called down to him, but he didn't answer, and I assumed he was just talking to himself or to one of his toys."

Jordan felt the chill of fear. He thought he already knew what she was going to say next. She told him she had run downstairs to find the little boy standing by the French doors into the garden, his hands pressed against the glass, his breath steaming the pane.

"He said, I had to open the door. The man had told him to. He was upset and pulling at the handle but, of course, it was locked and anyway, he doesn't know where the key is."

Penny turned to stare at Jordan. "I asked him what man, and he pointed into the garden. The movement sensor light wasn't lit, but there was someone out there. I'm sure of it. I saw him. He was running across the grass and then the bushes at the bottom by the fence were disturbed. I would have gone outside, but I didn't want to leave Harry and I wasn't going to take him out there when I didn't know what was going on."

"I'm bloody glad you didn't go out. How long was it after you arrived?"

"Not very long. I was only upstairs long enough to turn on Harry's heater, take my coat off and go to the toilet."

Possibly the person Harry had seen was already in the garden when they arrived. Maybe he was about to try to enter the house and was disturbed. Or he could have followed Penny home from the city and tried to enter once they were in. Both alternatives were chilling and no matter what the reason was, there was no innocent explanation.

"You haven't done anything?" he asked.

Penny shook her head. Now that he was home, she had given in to the shock and worry, and her hands shook as she held the glass. He wrapped his arms around her and let her lean against him.

"I'm here now, love," he said. "Don't worry. But we need to do something. We can't just ignore it. Will you be okay? I have to go outside and have a look at the lights. They should have come on, so that needs to be fixed. I'm going to call Stella and ask her to come over and we can have a look around. There's not much we can do immediately, but we'll look now so that tomorrow when the SOCO team comes, we can give them information. They won't be able to work in the dark. I don't think I need to call them tonight. He's gone, and I doubt he's going to come back." He paused. "Do you have any idea who it might have been? Any first impression. Don't overthink it. Just tell me your first idea."

"There was something about his figure, but it wasn't as if I knew him. It was definitely a man. Why are you calling Stella?"

"I just want to have a witness to everything. Just in case."

"In case what?"

He shook his head. "I just think it's best. Let's order the chicken and you sit here and have another drink while I check things outside."

"Jordan," she said.

"Yes, love."

"Be careful."

It was unusual for Penny to be so unnerved, and it made him angry. In his gut, he knew he had brought this trouble to his home and now he was going to have to fix it. But he wouldn't fix it alone. Although, he would have to cover his backside.

Chapter 46

Penny gasped when the doorbell rang, and Jordan was furious with the person who had reduced his normally calm and laid-back wife to such a nervous state.

He put a hand on her shoulder. "It'll be Stella, love."

"Yes, of course, I know, but…" She shook her head. "I'm okay. I can't believe how this has got to me. It was because Harry was talking to him. That scared me more than anything. What if he'd got in and…"

Jordan took hold of her hand. "He didn't, and Harry will have forgotten about this in the morning. The doors were locked, and you were okay. But I have to say this: anytime you are as worried as you were, then don't hesitate. Call the station, tell them who you are and they'll have someone here as quick as possible. We're at more risk than we used to be and if you tell them you're connected, they'll treat it as a priority."

"That sounds awful. We're just the same as everyone else."

"It would be nice to think so, wouldn't it? But it's not true and you shouldn't wait."

The bell sounded again, and Jordan shouted that he was on the way. Stella was dressed casually in jeans and a red Liverpool FC hoody, her blond hair tied back in a short ponytail.

She was puzzled. "What's happening, boss? You were a bit vague on the phone. Did you say you had an intruder?"

"Yes, we have, but only in the garden. The worry was that he was talking to Harry and trying to get access to the house. That was his aim rather than intending burglary, I reckon. If robbery had been his intention, he'd have shot off as soon as Penny arrived."

"Shit." She turned towards Penny, who was walking down from the kitchen. "You okay, Pens?" she said as she held out her arms to give the other woman a hug.

"I'm fine," Penny said. "I feel a bit of a wuss, to be honest. I wouldn't have thought this could have upset me so much. It's the baby… you hear such awful things." She began to cry.

The doorbell rang again, and the delivery of the spit-roast chicken eased the situation. Penny went off to set the table and pour drinks.

Jordan and Stella walked into the garden, which should have immediately been lit by the movement sensor, but it remained shadowed in the dusk. The three sensor lights had been broken. Glass and plastic lay on the grass and paving stones. Jordan had grabbed his torch and handed a second one to Stella. The damp soil showed disturbance and distinct footprints at the base of the fence. They took photographs of the indentations in the earth and covered the area with a plastic bin from the shed.

"So, are you going to tell me what's going on?" Stella said.

Jordan didn't bother trying to deny that there was a problem. He had asked for her help, and she couldn't do that without knowing all the facts.

He took a breath and told her about the report from the ballistics unit.

"Idiot," Stella said. "You should have told me. Even though you didn't want to believe it, you shouldn't have done anything without backup."

He couldn't argue, and he didn't even try.

"So, what's our first step?" Stella asked.

"SOCO are here tomorrow, although I'm not sure we'll get anything. But we will have evidence for the record if this goes anywhere. We need another word with Benno. I really want to know which house was being renovated. But apart from that, I don't have a clue where Pete might be. He said he was looking for somewhere to base the office, but I've no idea where."

"You can't trust anything he's said, though, can you? Are we sure that he's still working for that company?"

"I'd already thought of that. My betting is that no, of course he's not. I'll try to speak to the Met SIO on the case tomorrow. We really need to work together on this now."

"Will you tell them about your connection to him?"

"Once I know it's definitely him, of course. I have no choice. I don't think it'll be a problem. It's not like he's a relative or anything."

"You're pretty sure that he was the one in the garden, though, aren't you?"

"It's gut feeling as much as anything. Penny said she didn't recognise him, but she was panicked and she only had a glimpse. In a way, it's even worse if it wasn't because it means there's someone else out there who's trying to get at my family."

"As my granda says, let's not borrow trouble. Thing is, though, boss…" Stella said.

"Yes?"

"Why would he want to get to your lot? I mean, wouldn't you think he'd have legged it? I just don't understand why he would have come looking for you in the first place. Okay, he's on the run and needed to get rid of the gun, but why come here?"

"I honestly don't know."

Chapter 47

Jordan had wanted to take Penny to spend the day with her sister in Wavertree. She argued, insisted she was fine, and she had work to do at home. He told her it would make his life easier if he wasn't constantly worrying about whether she was okay, but the look she gave him ended the discussion. He wanted to remind her to lock the doors and take care if anyone came, but the memory of that look silenced him.

Detective Inspector Paul Keogh, the SIO in charge of the murder inquiry for the Met, reacted coolly at first when Jordan called him on Sunday morning. He grumbled that they should have spoken earlier and leaving it until what was nominally a day off wasn't winning the Liverpool force any friends. Jordan did what he could to smooth the ruffled feathers and gave him a precis of the robberies, murder, and subsequent manhunt that had delayed their reaction to the ballistics report.

It was when Jordan told him he thought he might know the suspect, that Pete had been in touch, and was possibly in Jordan's back garden the night before, that Keogh's interest was piqued. He suggested a Teams call within the hour and said he would be on his way up there as soon as it could be arranged.

Stella sat in on the computer conference from her own flat and John from his dad's place in Skelmersdale. This was the first time John had heard about his connection to the suspect and although he hardly reacted on the screen,

Jordan knew there would be questions later. In the end, the meeting was short, but the information was shocking. Paul Keogh was sending them details of when he would arrive in Merseyside the following day. His conversation was brief, to the point and punctuated with sighs and eye rolls. He finally leaned in close to the screen so that they had to focus on his face.

"DI Carr, this suspect, your friend, is in deep trouble. Not only do we believe he shot and killed his life partner, Tony Fletcher, but there is so much more." He paused. "Okay, a quick rundown, as it seems you haven't got the time in your busy day to read the reports we have sent you. If you have anything to add, please tell me now. Peter Roper is an addict. He is addicted to gambling. That much we are certain of because his friends, his other friends" – this was directed at Jordan – "were well aware of his struggles. He has run a successful company into the ground. Forensic accountants have been examining the books, and he is guilty of embezzlement and out-and-out theft from client accounts. He's deep in debt. Now, we can't know exactly what has happened between the two of them, but we do know that Tony Fletcher was shot and killed. Your chum, Peter the gambler, has disappeared. So, it doesn't take a genius to put the two things together, does it? As I said, if you know anything, then you need to tell me now."

Jordan reassured the London inspector that he had told him everything and they would give the Met all the help they needed from now on. However, none of them felt that the call ended amicably.

"Bloody hello, boss. What were you thinking?" John said. "That's last, that is. Did you know, Stel? Have I been kept in the dark here? What am I, some sort of sodding numpty? Can't be trusted?"

"It's not that, John," Jordan said. "Truly it's not. I didn't know what to do. It just didn't seem possible that Pete was involved and then, when it became clear that he actually was, I was going to tell you. This business with him coming to the house – well, probably him – has happened just now, and the situation changed quickly. I was hoping I could speak to him, but then he wasn't at the hotel. Well, of course he wasn't. He was too busy terrorizing my wife. He has never been there."

"No, and sorry, boss, speaking out of turn here, but you've been a proper div. You could have really landed yourself in the shit." John shook his head and sighed.

Jordan held up his hands in front of the screen. "I know, John. You really don't need to rub it in. So, I'm sorry. I don't think it's too late to fix things, though. We just need to find Pete. Also, I think we need to remember that, at the moment, this is all supposition."

"A bit more than that, boss," Stella said. "It was Pete's partner that was shot. The gun turned up here, as did your mate. There's the gambling and what have you. Come on, your head's still in the sand a bit."

Jordan chewed the inside of his lip and gave a deep sigh. "Yes, you're right. Of course you are. I've made a mistake, but I intend to fix it. First thing is to find out more about the gun. Then I've got to work out where the hell he's gone."

"You haven't got a clue though, have you?" Stella said.

"Not really, no. Looks like he's never been to the hotel and according to what we have just heard from DI Keogh, everything else he told me was untrue."

"So, why here? Does he have history here?"

Jordan shook his head. "Not that I know of."

"That's the first job then. See if we can find out why Liverpool."

"Yep, absolutely. I spoke to Nana and she couldn't remember the exact date he'd been to see her, but it was a few of weeks ago. I looked at the report on the homicide and it fits together. He spoke to her just before the body of his partner was found. I do have an idea about it, but I'd like to speak to her first. This stinks. Poor Nana, we need a statement. The Met can organise that, but I'll let her know first. I don't want to scare her."

"No, course you mustn't, but she's tough and they will need to interview her at some stage. So, before that, what's the first step?"

Jordan took a breath. "Back to Benno. I want to talk to him again about that gun. I'm not impressed by the statement we have. I don't believe him. He must remember where the skip was. We'll make him remember. Then we can look at CCTV. It's not much, but it's a start. John, I'm sorry. I wasn't deliberately holding stuff back. This has just developed. Also, I want you to find out who took the statement, they didn't do a good enough job. I'll have a word."

"Yeah. It's okay, boss," John said. "Don't worry. Let's just fix it, yeah?"

* * *

Benno's mother was flustered when they turned up at the house. "I thought you'd let him go," she said. "Why are you coming round mithering him?"

"He was released on bail and we have questions. I think you'd rather we did it here than at Copy Lane, but if you want, we can just take him back to the station," Stella told her.

"Does he need a solicitor?"

"That's up to you and him. You or his father can sit with him, or his uncle, anyone you like. The sooner we get on with this, the sooner we can go."

In the end, she allowed them access and showed them into the neat lounge with its three-piece suite and wall-mounted television.

"I'll fetch him. He's up in his room playing on his computer. He's still upset about what happened to his friend. How's Simon and that old man?"

Stella made a non-committal response and the woman turned away to yell up the stairs for her son to 'get your clothes on, there's police to see you'. Then she went to fetch her husband from the garden shed where, she told them, he was trying to keep busy and deal with all the upset. The glare she gave them as she left had Stella raising her eyebrows.

"You'd think we were the bad guys here, wouldn't you?" she said.

"It must be hard to deal with, though, when your kid goes off the rails," Jordan said.

"I guess so, but it's not our fault and they have to take some of the responsibility, surely."

Jordan's response was cut short by the parents who came to stand at the kitchen door, their faces drawn and worried, the father smelling of tobacco and oil. Benno clattered down the stairs, dressed in a pair of baggy tracksuit bottoms and a grey sweatshirt. In contrast to his mum and dad, he looked well rested and relaxed.

"Shit," he said. "What do you lot want? I thought I wouldn't see you again until court. This is harassment."

"No, it's not," Jordan said, "and we may well have to come back again. We are still dotting i's and crossing t's. As we told your mum, we can do this easily here or we can take you back with us."

Benno tried to hide the panic by pushing past them and throwing himself onto the settee. "Well, come on then, let's get on with it."

"I want to go back to when you found that gun, Benno," Jordan said.

"I told you it was in a skip."

"Yep, we got that. It was in your statement. What I want to know, though is how far down it was in the rubbish…"

"How d'ya mean?"

"Did you have to dig for it, or was it lying on the top?"

"I don't see why that matters."

"Well, I can assure it does, so how far down was it? Was it as if someone had tossed it in quickly and then gone away, or was it buried?"

"It wasn't far. What do you think I am? I'm not some scummer who goes digging in skips. I was looking to see if there was any good metal or anything. That's what Frank said I should do whenever I see them things, but I don't go digging in the filth."

"So, it was on the top?"

"Yeah, I said. Pretty near the top."

"Nothing at all on top of it?"

"Well, there might have been a couple of bags. I had to sort of shift them aside."

"Which is it, Benno? It can't have been on the top and under some bags," Stella said.

"Yeah, all right, I had to shift stuff around. That skip wasn't full anyway. It didn't look like they were using it just then. Sometimes the good stuff's at the bottom. Metal and that, it's heavy, innit."

"And were there men working on the site?" Jordan said.

"No. It was late. They'd finished for the day. They don't like you looking when they're there, so I make a note whenever I see one and go back."

"So, you do have a note of which house it was?" Stella said.

"Not a note, note, just in me head, like," Benno said, tapping at the side of his forehead.

"But you'll be able to tell us which one?" Jordan said.

"Yeah, maybe… I could try to show you on Google."

"Brilliant. Was there anything else with it?"

"Like what?"

"Clothes, bags, shoes? Anything like that?"

"Yeah, there was all sorts. It was a skip. You know what a skip is, don't you? It's where people put stuff."

"Ben, mind your mouth," Benno's father said and was rewarded with a huff.

"Well, of course there was other stuff in it," the lad muttered.

"So, do you know if the skip has been taken away?" Jordan said.

"I don't know, do I?" Benno said. "I never went back there. Honest, it spooked me a bit when Daz started going on about using the gun and then everything went mad. I couldn't think about anything else."

"Exactly when did you find it then?" Jordan asked.

"A bit back."

"Nope, that's not accurate enough," Stella said. She was hanging on to her temper by a thread. She knew she couldn't touch him, but the urge to give him a shake was overwhelming.

Benno's mum had run up the stairs and came back with a small tablet computer in her hand.

"You been in my room?" Benno said.

"Yes," she said. "I just thought it'd be quicker. For you to show them."

"Don't, yeah. I have to have my own space. Private, like. I've told you."

There was an awkward pause and Stella shook her head and moved to where Benno sat on the settee. "Stop buggering about," she said, "just show us. We haven't got all day for this." She took the tablet from the shocked hands of Mrs Midgely and thrust it towards her son.

Benno's fingers flew across the screen, and he held up the device with a close-up image on Google maps. "That's it, there. Doesn't show the work. They've knocked it all about since then, dug up the garden and all sorts. I reckon it was about ten days ago now. It was a Wednesday, so not last week but the one before. We did the first post office on the Friday."

He tried to inject some bravado into the statement, but the gasp from his mum brought colour flooding to his cheeks.

149

Jordan leaned over and took the location from the bottom of the screen. They left with the warning that they might well be back and for Benno to make sure he didn't go anywhere and to stick to his bail conditions. As they left, they heard Benno's dad slam out through the back door – presumably going back into hiding in the shed – and there was the thunder of feet on the stairs.

Chapter 48

The house being redeveloped in Crosby was one of the bigger properties. It wasn't far from where Jordan and Penny lived and as they drove from the Midgleys's house in Fazakerley, Jordan rang Penny. "Might as well nip in for coffee."

There was no answer.

Penny's car was in the drive, so he parked at the kerb. Jordan ushered Stella through the front door and called to his wife. He expected Harry to come charging down the hall and frowned at the quiet.

"She must have walked to the shops," he said. "Or down to the beach."

The pushchair was folded and propped in the hallway. They had been encouraging Harry to walk more, but they usually took his three-wheeler bike with them – little legs tired quickly and it was easier than picking him up. But the bike was in the corner of the living room.

There was no response to a second try on Penny's phone. Stella walked into the lounge and came back with the handset held in front of her.

"Guess she forgot it," she said.

Jordan tamped down the rising panic. "That's odd, but she might well be out with Lizzie." He dialled his sister-in-law's number.

As he waited for Lizzie to answer her phone, Stella strolled through to the kitchen.

"I'll make a brew," she said.

Penny and Harry were not with Lizzie, and she hadn't spoken to her sister. For a minute, Jordan couldn't speak. He couldn't verbalise the thoughts swirling in his mind. That would be to acknowledge the possibilities. He turned to look at Stella, who had come back and was watching him wide-eyed and serious.

"You need to come and have a look at this, boss."

It was a large kitchen, and it cost a lot of money to have it refitted. They'd saved up to have granite worktops and new cupboards, a stone sink, and stylish taps. It was a source of real pleasure for them both to cook in and have casual meals and breakfast. It was always spotless and gleaming.

There were no breakages, no blood, or sign of a struggle. The door was slightly open, as if someone had popped into the garden intending to come right back. Crumbs littered the worktop. A jar of peanut butter was tipped over on the table, the knife lying in a brown smear on the plastic mat. Harry's cup had rolled onto the floor, spilling sticky juice across the tiles. There was a mug half full of coffee on the worktop. It was so little, but it meant so much. It was unthinkable that Penny would go out and leave the kitchen in such a mess.

Jordan stepped out through the sliding doors and into the garden. He ran to the end where the SOCO team had left the bin after they made moulds of the footprints. The ground didn't appear to have been disturbed since then. He dragged open the shed door. It was the same shabby, messy space as always. He strode to the side gate, which was unlocked and slightly open. Inquisitive and adventurous Harry meant this gate was always locked with a bolt at the top. Anyone wanting access would need to reach over to unlock it.

Jordan's stomach was churning, his heart thumped, and he thought he might vomit. Desperately, because it had to be done, he dragged open the garage door. Penny had been depressed after Harry arrived and sometimes Jordan had worried about her being on her own with her mood so low, but they had come through it and she had been fine for years now. He didn't expect to find her body there, and although he blew out a tightly held breath when he looked at the empty space, relief was quickly replaced with the greater fear.

Back in the house, Stella had checked all the rooms upstairs and when Jordan came back, she simply shook her head.

Penny wasn't there. She had left or been taken unexpectedly, and his son was with her.

"I'll raise the alarm," Stella said as she pulled out her Airwave set.

"No, wait. Just hang on a minute."

"You're kidding, boss. We need to act quickly. Okay, I understand you don't want to make a fuss, but if she turns up with a lolly ice and sand on her shoes, we can all just have a laugh about it."

"It's not that. I don't give a shit about being embarrassed," Jordan said.

"Well, what then?"

"If we put this out, then we're going to be dragged into protocol and procedure. You know how that will be. I'll be sidelined. I can't let that happen. It's down to me to find them. Now. It has to be me." He paused. "And you, if you'll help."

"Of course, I'll help, but if we put the call out, they'll pull out all the stops. Start an all-points alert, get a *'be on the lookout for'* on social media and the news."

"And if Pete has them, as we are both thinking, that's going to panic him, and we don't know how he'll react. It's highly likely he's killed once, Stel. What has he got to lose by doing it again? I need to find them now."

"But you don't even have a clue where to look. You've got nothing."

She was right, and he had no response. He paced back and forth along the hall, running his hand through his hair and clawing at his scalp.

He stopped and drew in a deep breath. "Right, call John, give him a quick rundown, and ask him to meet us at Copy Lane. I'll take a quick drive down to the shore. Just in case. Ask him to find out about CCTV everywhere in the area. Let's start with a two-mile radius. Can you see if there are any security or doorbell cams locally so we can view the footage right away now? Knock at all the houses round here. Not next door. I know she hasn't got one and the house across the street, they're away, so don't waste time with them."

"It's too much, boss. We need help."

"We haven't got time. You know it will take too long to get a team together, mobilise door knockers, all of that. The kettle is still warm. The coffee in the cup as well. She can't have been gone long. We can find her if we move now. Come on, mate. Help me."

Chapter 49

Jordan broke the speed limit on the drive to the riverfront before leaping out of the car, leaving the door open. There were a couple of dog walkers, several joggers, and a group of lads kicking a ball about on the wide, flat sands. The iron men sculptures stared out across the estuary, unmoved by the drama in his life. He had known she wouldn't be there but had to look. He spun the car in the road, mounting the kerb at both sides and drove back to the house.

Stella was knocking on doors and running along paths without waiting for answers. It seemed illogical, but it was a good use of time. If there was no answer, then she was already at the next house and if there was a response, she could talk to more than one person at once over the spaces that made up the drives. An official house-to-house would be more controlled – introductions and polite questions, the handing over of calling cards. She was holding her warrant card in her hand the whole time, but the further away from Jordan's home she went, the less likely it was that any footage would be useful.

Jordan started at the houses on the same side as his own. Two doors away, the little old lady was offended when she told him 'no, she didn't have a camera, but would he like to come in for a brew' and he ran back down the path without a word. He was halfway down the next drive when Stella called him, waving 'come here' hands in the air. He arrived at the house as she was stepping inside. There was no way to avoid the introductions, though every word felt like time wasted. Fortunately, being a six-foot-tall black man with a beautiful wife and a cute son had brought them some notice, and the grey-haired man ushered them through to his dining room when Stella was halfway through the explanation.

"Aye, I saw them. I thought it was odd, the little boy crying and all." The man logged on to his computer and opened the app for his security camera. "There you go. The last hour. See. It was the car that activated it. I have it pointed at the road to catch the buggers who let their dogs crap by my gate." He pointed at the surprisingly clear video. "That car. That stopped outside your house."

They leaned forward to watch as a white Ford Focus drove in front of the camera, executed a three-point turn, and pulled to a stop in front of Jordan's gateway. The driver climbed out and they had a view of his head and shoulders as he glanced back and forth and then squeezed past Penny's car in the drive. They lost sight of him as he walked to the wooden gate to the back garden. By this time, he was out of the shot.

"Is it him?" Stella asked.

"I think so. We don't get much of a look," Jordan said.

"Hang on." As he spoke, the neighbour rewound the image and froze it at the point where the driver left the car.

"It's him. I'm sure it is," Jordan said.

"Any chance you can let us have a copy of this, mate?" Stella said.

"Of course." The old guy looked a bit smug. "I should be able to do the still. It's a screen grab and I've just got the hang of those…" He hesitated. "But if you want to do it, feel free."

"Tell you what, can you just send us the whole video so we can enhance it and maybe make out the reg?" Stella said.

"Give me the address. I'll shoot that off."

"Did you see him come out?" Jordan said.

"I heard the alarm again and had a quick look out the window. She was carrying the little boy, and the driver sort of ushered her into the back. Like I said, it looked a bit off. I'm really kicking myself, I should have done something. Hey, mate" – he reached a hand to touch Jordan on the shoulder – "I hope she's okay, your missus, and the kid, like."

"Thanks. Did that record when they left?"

"Aye, it did. Here you go. Might be upsetting, like – sorry."

They watched Penny clamber into the back seat with a hand raised to protect Harry's head as she bent to enter the car. Pete slammed the door, leaned down and said something through the window, slid into the driver's seat and drove away. The view of his face was much better and left no doubt about identification. Jordan covered his eyes with his hands and blew out a breath. Then he straightened his shoulders and turned to the neighbour.

"We'll need to come back to take your statement at some point," he said.

"Sound. No problem."

As Jordan and Stella left, Jordan spoke to John in Copy Lane. "There's a video coming through. That's the car we're looking for. No full plate number, but there's a partial. See what you can do and get on to traffic and ask them to be on the lookout. Just a person of interest at the moment." He paused. "John, if it's spotted, tell them not to stop it, but just to follow. I don't want him panicked."

"On it, boss. Are you coming in?"

"We're on the way. Let us know if he's seen though, and we'll be after him."

"Thank heavens for crapping dogs, eh, boss," Stella said. "But, boss. What's this all about? Okay, I get we think he's the person who dumped the gun in the skip. Weird, I agree, and we would always have been involved, helping the Met. But Penny, what's that for? Have you got history with this bloke that I don't know about?"

Jordan shook his head. "I knew him way back when we were at school. We were friends but not really close and then we lost touch, as you do. I've spoken to Nana Gloria and there was some sort of 'where are they now' article in the school magazine. I remember them asking permission. There were a couple of doctors, a TV producer, stuff like that. It was meant to show students they could have anything if they committed. I was flattered, to be honest, so I said yes and told myself I was doing it to help the kids. It was to help my bloody ego. That's what it was and now, look. He only met Penny a few days ago when he came to dinner."

"Hmm. That's a bit shit, then. Thing to remember, though, is she didn't look upset, Jordan. I know Harry was crying, but Penny wasn't struggling or anything. She just got in the car. She wasn't hurt as far as we could see. Okay, she wasn't exactly laughing, but it really looked as though she went voluntarily."

Jordan nodded his agreement, but her words hadn't helped much, and her observations just added to the mystery.

Chapter 50

John had his head down over the screen but stood and came to meet them when they arrived. "I've found the car, I think. It's registered to a small local rental firm. I've been trying to raise the office on the phone, but it just goes to voicemail. Do you want me to shoot over there?"

"Not a lot of point if they're not answering the phone," Jordan said. "I expect they're closed. See if you can find a home address for the owner. Mind you, we know who hired it, so really, we just need an address for Pete. He must have given one. It'll probably be false, of course. Everything else up to now has been a bloody lie. It would be useful to know when he rented it, though."

"Do you want to call Kath in, boss?" Stella said. "You know she's brilliant on the CCTV searches."

Jordan stared at her and bit his bottom lip. "Give her a bell. Make sure she knows that right now we're working off grid and we want to keep it quiet for the time being. Leave it up to her. There could be repercussions. You both know that, don't you?"

"Of course," John said. "I agree with Stel, though. It would be easier if we had all the help we can get."

Jordan rubbed a hand over his jaw. "All the help and me stuck in a room chewing my nails because they think I'm too close to it. I can't, John. Not yet. I just can't."

With a shrug of his shoulders, John went back to his desk and Stella called Kath, who told them she'd be with them within the hour.

For a while there was quiet, just the click of the keyboards and the subdued noise drifting in from the station. After a while, Stella knocked on Jordan's open office door and brought a mug of coffee to where he sat staring at the video from the neighbour's camera. "Kath's here, boss, she's on it now."

"Nothing from Traffic?" Jordan asked, and she shook her head.

He turned away from the screen to sip at the drink. The phone in his jacket pocket vibrated. He dragged it out and frowned as he clicked to open the video file.

Penny was trying hard not to cry. She cradled their son and mouthed 'sorry' before the image clicked off and the screen returned to blank grey.

Stella hadn't seen what Jordan had seen, but his expression chilled her. "What. What was it?"

"Penny, it was Penny and the baby." Before he said more, an incoming message pinged.

> *I need your help. Wait for a call. Don't attempt to trace this phone. You won't be able to and you don't want anything to happen to your lovely wife and this cute little lad, do you? Let's just keep this between us. Yes?*

Jordan held out the phone.

"Shit, what the hell?" Stella said. "Boss, you need to call this in. We need help. You're going to need a negotiator. This is some sort of hostage situation. You can't handle this on your own."

"No!"

Stella stepped back as he raised his voice. He'd never been so agitated. It was understandable, but he was close to the edge, and she didn't want to be a witness to him tipping over. John's chair screeched as he stood and strode over from his desk.

"What's going on?" he asked.

Stella handed over the phone and as he took it, the incoming call tone sounded. Jordan snatched it back.

Jordan didn't put the call on speaker, but they could hear enough of the conversation. First came the threat. Then came the demand. As the call ended suddenly, Jordan placed the handset carefully onto his desktop, pushed his chair back and took the few steps to his window. He braced his hands on the frame for a moment and then drew back his fist and thumped it hard against the wall. The thin plaster dented, and a small cork board clattered to the floor.

"Shit, shit, shit!"

Chapter 51

Jordan paced back and forth in the incident room. His fists were clenched and his expression thunderous. He glowered at the notice board. Nobody had anything to say to make him feel any better.

Pete Roper had asked for the impossible. Even if he had been willing, there was no chance of Jordan interfering in the Met's investigation. The kidnapper had asked for a rundown of where their enquiries were and what the next steps were likely to be. He wanted details deleted from the Police National Computer and the HOLMES 2 system and the all-ports alert to be cancelled. He wanted the gun to disappear and if that wasn't possible, then for there to be interference in the evidence chain to make it inadmissible if there was ever a court case. Then he demanded another car with no trace on it. He said that he would be back with directions of where to bring the vehicle when his other demands had been met.

All of this was out of the question. It was so ludicrous, Stella had voiced the thought that he was 'away with the fairies'. It would have been laughable if it were not for the horrible situation with Penny and Harry.

"I can't believe he actually thinks you'll help him get away with this, boss," John said. He asked the same question as Stella had a short while before. "Has he got something on you? I realise you probably don't want to say, but if we're going to help you out here, you have to be honest with us."

"There's nothing," Jordan said. "I was boringly well-behaved at school. My mum and Nana saw to that. I didn't even pinch sweets from the pick'n'mix. But for God's sake, he doesn't need anything, does he? He's got Penny and Harry. That bloody article made much of the fact that we were together and happy. It was all part of the message that things can be good even if you come from a sink estate and have to struggle. So, that said, the only thing I can do is find the bastard. Now. And when I do, I'll kill him."

"No, you won't, boss," Stella said.

He stared at her for a moment, frowned, and turned away to stalk across the room to where Kath was desperately searching for the hired car.

She had begun the look for traces of it on the local traffic cameras, but if he was driving on minor roads, he wouldn't be picked up by those. Without issuing requests for help, they were missing out on the chance of seeing the vehicle on shops' CCTV, bus cameras, or dash cams. The Traffic cars were alerted, but it was all low key. Barely more than a casual mention and with so few patrols around the quieter roads of Crosby, there had been nothing. There had been no media posts and although the feedback from those was often overwhelming and largely useless, it would have been better than the nothing they were working with now. Kath was frustrated and felt panic rising as time passed. Of all the times to let them down, this was the worst.

She pushed back from the desk. "Boss, we can't do it like this. We should be pulling out all the stops. It's your missus, your little lad. The media should be flooded with alerts and images and alarms."

"And then he'll hurt them and run," Jordan said. "He's got nothing to lose. We all know he's killed his partner. We haven't yet seen the details of why, and right now it doesn't matter to me. He's guilty, that's what's important. If the whole force is out looking for him and the radio, telly, and internet are swamped with it, he'll panic. I can't have him desperate. I have to make him think he's got a chance to get away with this, for now at least."

Stella listened to the back and forth as she watched, again, the car drive away from Jordan's house on the neighbour's video. She spun her chair away from the desk. "What if he hasn't gone out onto the main roads at all? That's why we can't find him. We've assumed that he took Penny and drove off. He might still be in the area. He lied about where he was staying, so there's no guarantee he's gone to the city centre. He could easily still be in Crosby."

There was silence. Jordan crossed to the noticeboard. The images of Benno, Daz and Stick had been taken down and laid on the table. He picked up the one of Benno.

"What's the latest image we have of the refurbishment property?" he asked.

Kath turned back to her computer to bring up Street View. "It's last year, boss. Looks as though they had just started the work. It's still pretty much undisturbed, but they've put up metal fencing and there's one of those mobile toilet things. I've pinged you the picture."

Jordan took out his phone and swiped and enlarged the image until it blurred, then pinched his fingers across the screen to resize it. He clicked back to the image of his wife, caught in the moment as she mouthed an apology.

The tears glinting in her eyes tore at his heart, but he pushed the emotion aside and examined the shot, zooming closer to the periphery of the picture, peering closely at what should have been incidental.

"Okay, Stella, you come with me. We need to have a look at that place. See just how far along it all is. It's less than two weeks since Benno fished the gun from the skip."

"I'll come, boss," John said.

"Take me with you, John," Kath said.

They all turned to look at her. It wasn't very long since she had her knee replaced.

She straightened her shoulders. "I'm fine, better than ever. I hardly even limp now. You can't leave me here while you all go buggering off to Crosby. Come on, be fair."

"You're with me," John said, and the team barrelled out of the station.

Chapter 52

Traffic was light at this time on a Sunday evening and they didn't need to use the integral blue lights. John was close behind as they turned at Thornton and sped down Moor Lane and through Great Crosby. Instinct took Jordan weaving through the area and his route passed his own home. Nearer to the beach, they joined wide roads of spacious villas with brick walls and fancy gateposts. Lots of the houses were converted into care homes and their historically large gardens given over to blocks of low-rise flats.

They pulled into the kerb around the corner from the front entrance to the site. "What's the plan, boss?" John said.

Jordan ran a hand over his face. "I don't want us going in mob handed."

"Not much chance of that, boss. There's just four of us," Stella said.

"Okay, what I mean is, let's take it steady at first. John, there's an alley down the back. See if you can get all the way through. Do you reckon you'll be up for it if you have to climb, Kath?"

"I came, boss. I told you, I reckon I'm fine. Anyway, I guess there's only one way to find out."

"Okay. Stel and I will go down the front of the house. I want to see if there's any obvious activity. Keep in touch. I reckon text messaging is best right now until we find out what's what. We're looking for lights, signs of breaking and entering, anything at all that might tell us he's been there, maybe is there now, or nothing at all. It's all we've got right now, and it's not much more than just a feeling, but the windows on the video of Penny were these. I'm convinced of it. I need to do this."

"Back here in ten, yeah?" John said.

"Yes, if nothing shows. Try not to be seen."

"Well, yeah!" John said.

"Sorry," Jordan said, and he put a hand on the younger man's shoulder. "I'm wound pretty tight."

"Of course you are, mate, how could you not be? But we're on this and if he's there, if they're there, we'll get them out."

There was no gate, but a panel of Heras fencing had been wedged between the brick posts. It was dirty and rusty in places with a 'Keep Out' notice fixed to the crisscrossed wires. Empty takeaway boxes and plastic bags had collected around the base of it.

"Doesn't look as though this has moved regularly in a while," Stella said.

Jordan crouched and pointed to a couple of grooves in the dirt lying on the path.

"Benno was telling porkies. I don't reckon there have been builders on site recently. But somebody was. He was in here to see what he could filch. The skip looks as though it's been there a long time, and the rubbish has sort of settled. He obviously broke in and rooted around for anything he could find," Stella said. "Look at this, though." She shone the light from her torch on the sign and the address for 'contact in an emergency'. "Fletchers. That's him, isn't it? That's the dead bloke's name. So, it's his company, well, theirs – his and Pete's. That explains a lot." She photographed the notice, which included the phone number and address.

They dragged the makeshift gate aside just enough to squeeze through and then replaced it. Behind the tall yew hedge, the garden was overgrown and weedy. The light from streetlamps glittered on standing water. Rubble and lumps of building debris littered the space.

"Doesn't look like a busy building site to me," Jordan said. "You're right, I reckon. It's abandoned."

"Well, we know now that he's gone bust. But he knew that this place was just sitting empty. Near you. That has to be the reason he was here," Stella said.

They moved quietly towards the sad, empty building, aiming the light from their torches at the ground directly in front of their feet.

A text from John's phone told them he and Kath had clambered over the wall and reached the back of the property. It was all in darkness.

Jordan's phone vibrated in his pocket, and he dragged it out to peer at the screen. The number was withheld. He held the handset between them and turned on the voice recorder. It wasn't legal and wouldn't be admissible in court, but if this was Pete, he wanted a record.

"This is just what I expected." He recognised the voice immediately. "Don't know what you think you're doing.

You're supposed to be sorting things for me. But there we are. I thought you might try something like this. So, now you're here, see if you can get in. I've heard all about how clever you are, how resourceful. Let's see how you do. There could be a surprise. No, scrap that. There is a surprise. Maybe if you don't move things along, there'll be another one later, a bigger one."

The hairs on Jordan's neck prickled, and his stomach lurched. "Where are you, Pete? Let's meet up, let's talk about all this. Just let my family go and I'll help you."

"That's what I asked you to do. But you have to do it now, quickly, or there'll be more surprises. Don't mess me about. Hurry up, Cracker, you haven't got much time."

The line went dead.

"We need to get in there. Now. We don't need a warrant. I'm sure there is a risk to life." As he yelled at Stella, Jordan ran across the weedy gravel towards the big front door. It was covered with a security grill which was screwed into the frame and fastened with a hefty lock. The windows were covered with anti-theft screens, secured and vandal-proofed.

"How does he know we're here, boss?" Stella said.

"How the hell do I know? The point is, he does." He peered around, looking for a way in, and spotted the red light under the eaves. It was pointless, but he couldn't help himself. He flicked a two fingered gesture towards the camera.

"We can't shift this, not without equipment. We need to call for help and get a bolt cutter or something."

John texted to let them know there was nothing to see in the rear garden and they were now trying to access the house.

There was no need now for quiet, and Jordan shouted into his phone. "Now, John, we need to get in there."

Chapter 53

The front of the house was impenetrable with bars and barriers over every entrance. They ran down a side passage, splashing through dirty pools of water. Creeping vines grabbed at their ankles and overhanging tree branches snatched and tore at them as they battered their way through. A huge builder's bag of sand had been dumped at the end of the narrow walkway. It had split, and part of the contents spewed out across a crazy paving patio. Jordan stretched his legs to clamber over and then turned back to help Stella. She was shorter and ended up on all fours, crawling across the dirty wet plastic. She got to her feet, slapping and swiping at the wet sand sticking to her clothing and hair.

John and Kath were several metres along the paved area, kneeling on the ground with Kath shining a torch to where John was working. She turned and beckoned to Jordan and Stella.

"There's a window here. It's a cellar skylight. There's a window well and then a metal grill in front of it, but it's rusty. John reckons he might be able to shift it. He's got a crowbar we found in the garden."

Jordan ran to the corner and peered down the path at the other side of the house, hoping to find a coal chute cover that might have been overlooked and would be easier to break into. If one had been there, it had been bricked up. There were no windows, the French doors which, in better days, would have looked out onto the spacious garden were boarded and sealed. If John couldn't break through into the cellar, they weren't getting in.

There was no choice. They had to do this. Pete's comments had carried a clear threat; before, it had been just an idea, not much more than a gut feeling, but now he was certain that Penny and Harry were inside and needed to be found, and quickly. Jordan didn't allow himself to think about what state they might be in because then he would lose all control.

He had to hold himself together. He paced back and forth, his fists clenching and unclenching. There was the clatter of metal hitting concrete, and he ran to look down into the space around the cellar window. One of the bars had fallen to the ground and another was loosened at the base, John pulling and twisting it. Bits of stone broke loose and cascaded into the pit and, with a sudden lurch, a second bar came free. There was no room for Jordan to help. He offered to take over, but John shook his head.

"Nearly there, boss. This next one is already loose, and I reckon then I'll be able to smash the glass. One of the girls should be able to get in."

"All the doors are barred though, John."

"I know, but at least there would be someone inside and I'll keep on with this. Once all the bars are out, even a fat slob like me will fit through and we'll be able to do something with all of us. It's getting easier the more mortar that comes off. It's old and crumbly."

The bar came away with a sharp jerk and John threw it aside. Stella was already taking off her bulky outer coat, ready to climb through the window.

Kath held out a pair of leather gloves. "Here, take these. They'll protect your hands."

Stella looked up. "Oh, but these are dead nice. They'll be ruined."

Kath didn't bother to answer. She simply raised her eyebrows and pushed the gloves into Stella's hands.

She had to squirm and wriggle, but she made it through. Later, she'd suffer pain from the bruises and scratches on her belly, but for now, they didn't even register.

John passed a torch through to her and they watched the cone of light flicker over the flagstone floor of the basement room. Then John went back to dragging and prying at the metal bars.

Jordan had Stella on speakerphone. She gave them a commentary until the signal was lost and she had to shout to them as she found the rotting wooden stairs. She squealed as a tread cracked under her feet but carried on, testing each step before putting her weight on it. A heavy door blocked the top of the creaking flight and there was a moment of panic when she thought it was locked. They could just make out the noise as she grunted and swore, and the slam as it flew back and hit the wall. Once out of the cellar, the signal came back and she could communicate again.

"That door was just swollen with the damp. Jesus, it stinks in here. Right, I'm moving through a kitchen and down the hall." Her footsteps echoed in the empty space.

Another bar in the window came loose, leaving just two more and enough room for Kath to scrabble through.

"Shall I go now?" Kath asked.

"No, hang on. Wait until Stella sees what's what," Jordan said.

They heard the scuttle as Stella began to run, and her gasping cry.

"What, what is it, Stel? What's there?" Jordan said.

"Oh, boss. Boss, we need an ambulance. Call them now."

Chapter 54

Kath was already dialling. Jordan knelt on the floor, shining his torch through the broken window and into the dark cellar.

They heard Stella coming, her feet on the stairs and her murmuring as she crossed the flags towards them.

"Be careful. Mind his neck," she said. Jordan reached down and gripped the bundled sleeping bag with his son curled inside.

"He's breathing, boss. He's warm and there's no blood or nothing."

Stella was still inside the cellar and had realised by now that she had no way to climb out. It didn't matter. She had brought the baby, and his dad was holding him close, pulling at the quilted fabric, feeling for his pulse, crooning and rocking him with tears streaming down his face. The little boy stirred and coughed, and they heard the wail of the siren in the distance.

John turned away from Jordan and his son and leaned closer to where Stella was watching through the window. He spoke quietly. "Penny?"

Stella shook her head. "I haven't been upstairs because all I could think of was getting Harry out of there. I'll go back now. Can Kath come, do you think? Also, grab something for us to stand on to get out afterwards. Some blocks or something as there's nothing in here, and I can't reach to climb up."

Jordan was cradling Harry close to him, as he leaned towards John and Stella at the window. He glanced up as they heard Kath shouting directions to the paramedics who were scrambling over the debris.

As the medics appeared around the corner and reached to take the baby, Jordan turned to John with panicked tears in his eyes.

"Go, boss. You go with Harry. If Penny's here, we'll find her. We'll get her out and look after her and we'll keep you informed. Just go, yeah."

"I can't," Jordan said. "Not until I know."

"Boss, you're too big to get through this hole. What are you going to do, just stand here while your little lad goes in the ambulance on his own? Penny wouldn't want you to do that."

* * *

It was quiet in Alder Hey Hospital. There were a few children crying or sitting silently beside worried and harassed parents, drawn and haggard, sipping at cardboard cups. Jordan was in a cubicle, tense and tired, next to a narrow couch where Harry was snuggled under a blanket.

Stella hovered near the entrance. "Can I come in, boss?"

Jordan stood and hugged her. "Come on in. He's asleep. They've taken blood, run some tests. He woke up a while ago and had a big drink. He's had a pee. It's all good. He can go home as soon as the blood results are back, but they reckon he's been given an overdose of something, possibly just a sleeping tablet. But all his vitals are good."

"Shit, poor little sod."

By now Jordan had gone back to sit beside his son, squeezing his hand, stroking his hair. Stella stepped closer, and told him that she and Kath had gone back into the house. He already knew they hadn't found Penny. John had sent a text. The place was dirty and damp except for the room where the little boy had been wrapped in the sleeping bag and laid on a mattress. The impression was that Pete had been living there. She showed him images of the small stove in the corner, an electric kettle, and a folding bed that had formed a makeshift campsite. The electricity was on, and they had already put in an enquiry to find who was paying the bills.

"Lizzie's on her way," Jordan said. "She's going to stay with Harry and I've told them she can take him home when he's ready. I had to tell her what was going on and she's upset, but she's as tough as her sister and holding it together."

"Don't you want to stay with him?" Stella said.

"Yes, of course I do. But I can't. I have to find Penny. She'll be desperate about the baby. I have to get this bastard and make him pay for what he's done to us. If he's killed his partner, that's something else, but I've got to get him for Harry and Penny, and for me."

John and Kath were still at the big old house in Crosby, searching the skip by the light of their torches. It was a filthy job but if Pete had been living there, then it was possible he had thrown something away that would help.

"We've got the DI from London arriving in a few hours, boss," Stella said. "You're going to have to open this up."

He knew she was correct. If he didn't find his wife before the morning, then the chances were that it would be snatched from his hands. He shook his head.

Lizzie put her head round the curtain. "They said I could come in," she said. Her eyes were swollen and reddened, and her face was drawn, but she walked over to Harry and kissed his cheek. "He'll be fine with me. I spoke to the doctor. They reckon he can go home when he's had another drink and they've given him the final once over. Find Penny, Jordan, just find my sister and bring her home."

Stella had brought Jordan's car to the hospital, and he let her drive them back to Crosby. "I'm going to read the report about the homicide," he said. "Up to now, I've scanned bits of it. Maybe if I'd done the job properly, I could have avoided all this."

"And just when were you going to do that? We've been flat out, and it wasn't our case."

"Well, okay, I still feel as though I've cocked up. Now I need to understand what went on. I'll read it out to you, if you like."

"Yeah, go on. I always like a bedtime story." Stella laughed. "Not much chance of bed, but anyway, I'll have the story."

"I really appreciate what you're doing, mate. You and the others."

"Oh, shut up. Stop blethering on. You'd do the same for us. Anyway, I'm ready. Start at the beginning. Once upon a time."

Chapter 55

Jordan was still reading when Stella pulled the car into the entrance of the building site. Much of what he'd been told had been true. Pete Roper had been in property development. The company had done well for a while and then money began to leak out of the accounts. By the time Antony's murdered body was found on waste ground beside the Thames, the company was bankrupt. Forensic accountants had already discovered that large amounts of money had been withdrawn regularly and were painstakingly following the convoluted trail. They were checking for anything else, such as money laundering, that Pete may have been involved in. It was nothing new to them and just a matter of time before everything was clarified.

DI Keogh was convinced that the financial crime must have led to Antony's death and that Pete Roper was responsible. With the discovery of the gun, that was no longer in any real doubt. For the Liverpool cops, the issues were different. He'd killed his partner. He was possibly linked to organised crime. No doubt he was a crook, but more importantly, right now, he had Penny.

Back at the house, John had a small pile of crumpled and dirty papers on the wall in the garden. "These are receipts with recent dates on. All for food except for a couple from a chemist where he bought some Piriton syrup. It might be a good idea to let the hospital know. That could well be what he's given your lad," he said to Jordan and Stella when they arrived.

"I'll do that, boss," Stella said. "Give me your Lizzie's number and she can tell the doc."

Jordan handed over his phone and picked up the papers to look through them.

"Brilliant, John, thanks for that. Right, what we need to do now is get that bloody camera down," he said.

"I don't see why that matters now, boss. He knows we've been here, and he achieved his objective," John said.

"Yes, I know, but that thing obviously feeds to his phone. I've researched them, because I was going to fit one at home. If we're lucky, it has a removable SD card in it. We can access the recordings. We can see what he did, but more importantly, it might have recorded him and my wife."

"There's some old ladders stacked behind the shed." John was already jogging over the bedraggled garden.

The wood was old and rotten. It was clearly unsafe, but John insisted on climbing up to the eaves. Jordan footed the ladder, and the others lit the way with torches. Halfway up, two of the rungs cracked and split, but he hung on to the sides and continued to climb. Once there, he tugged at the camera and leaned to look down at them.

"Jesus, John. Don't do that," Kath said. "Just get the thing and come down. Don't be jigging about and stuff."

"I'm sound," he said. "You move your torch over a bit so I can see this thing better. I just need to know, Jordan, do we need the whole thing or does anyone know how I get this card thing out?"

"There'll be a little slot," Jordan said. "It might be hard to find up there. Can you bring it down?"

"I can try, but it's well fixed. Does it matter if I break it?"

"I don't think so."

Kath closed her eyes as he tugged on the plastic device. "Tell me when he's down," she said. "I can't look."

John gave a sudden jolt and even Jordan gasped as the ladder wobbled and bits of wood and dirt cascaded around them. "Leave it, mate. Come down. It's too dangerous."

"No bloody way. I'm almost there. It's giving up."

"So's this ladder. It's breaking apart. You're going to end up on your back. Come down."

John let out a cry, and the steps wobbled again, but he twisted to show them the camera in his hand. "Got the bugger." He tucked it inside his jacket and began the clamber back down. When he was just over a metre from the bottom, the old wood finally gave way depositing him in a heap.

"Oh shit," Kath said. "Lie still, are you hurt? Have you broken anything?"

John waved her away. "I'm fine. I'm going to have a bruise on my arse, but I'm fine. Here!" He held out the device to the boss.

Jordan turned it over and round, searching for the telltale slot. "Yes." He pulled out the little card and grinned at the others. "That's stage one. Now we just have to read the thing."

"Will it go in a phone?" Stella said.

"I hope so. If not, I've got an adaptor at home. Let's see."

They went back to Jordan's car, where it was warmer and lighter.

It was a fiddly job but in just a few minutes the phone's file manager had located the footage, and they were watching the front of the house on the little screen.

There were birds, blowing leaves, and a couple of passing joggers, which all activated the device, but there was also Penny and Harry being pushed into the front entrance by Pete Roper. Penny had obviously realised that something was very wrong and had begun to fight back, trying to kick out at the man and grabbing at the doorposts one handedly. But she was handicapped trying to protect the little boy and minimize his distress. Her bravery and the abuse were almost too much, but Jordan forced himself to watch. They went inside and the metal cover slammed shut.

For a while there was minimal movement, darkness fell, and the streetlights illuminated part of the front garden.

Jordan skimmed past the coloured graphs until a longer section of activity showed on the slider at the bottom of the screen.

Pete came out of the front door and a short while later, a dark-coloured Jaguar pulled up to the front door.

"That's why we can't find him. He's changed vehicles," Stella said.

They heard Jordan growl deep in his throat as Penny was dragged kicking and squirming from the house. She tried with everything she had not to be pushed into the back of the car. Pete lashed out with the flat of his hand to her face. Jordan's knuckles were white as he gripped the phone. She was forced inside and onto the floor and the door slammed. Pete turned to secure the house and drove off, leaving a drugged child in the house and taking his desperate mother away.

John laid a hand on Jordan's shoulder. "We'll get him, boss. We could see the make and model and a partial plate. Listen, it's time now to declare this an abduction and to let everyone know what's going on. He's out there somewhere and with everyone on the lookout for that car, we're going to have him."

The video of his wife struggling with all that she had not to be taken had torn at his heart, and all Jordan could

175

do was nod. Already all three were active, raising the alarm and getting the word out.

"I'll drive us back to the station," Stella said. "We need to be there when the reports come in."

Chapter 56

Notifications had gone out over the Airwave system and by the time they arrived at Copy Lane there was a hubbub of activity. Extra cars from nearby forces had been called in and were on their way to trawl the city. Beat coppers were calling in for instructions and as they walked down the corridor, every colleague they encountered offered help and insisted they would stay on duty until Penny was found. DCI Josh Lewis called and asked to be kept informed, and said that he was ready to come in if there was anything he could contribute. Nobody could think of anything, but they agreed to keep him across the situation. He had suggested that when it was all over, he and Jordan would need to talk. At this point, that made no impression on anyone.

Kath had contacted Violet Purcell, and the sound of her shoe heels could be heard thudding down the corridor as she ran to the incident room. She threw off her coat and logged on to her computer before she took the time to greet anyone.

The uniformed PC, Sharon Taylor, who had been catching up on paperwork at the end of her shift, had quietly commandeered a desk in the corner of the room and was skimming through PNC reports, looking for information about stolen Jaguars.

It wasn't long before she raised a hand. "Think I've found the car, boss. Nicked from the city centre earlier today, well yesterday now, I guess. I've got the owner's details if you need them."

"Is he local?" Jordan said. "Any record?"

"No, he's Welsh; was just visiting. He's gone back to Llanberis now."

"Okay, just make a note," said Jordan. "Find out if there were any cameras nearby, although we know who took it, but he might have had help. Well done. Let everyone know the full registration."

Jordan couldn't sit still. He was torn between a need to be out in the city looking for Penny and the knowledge that he was better waiting until he had a sighting of the car. Every few minutes, he was swept by a wave of nausea. If he lost his wife, he didn't believe he would be able to carry on. There was Harry, but without Penny, nothing would make sense. Stella brought him coffee. She didn't speak because there was nothing for her to say that would make any difference. She laid a hand on his arm, and it was enough.

Lizzie messaged to let him know their little boy had been discharged, and she was on the way home with him.

The traffic patrol officers on the motorways were alerted. The whole country was on standby. There was no reason to think Pete would try to take Jordan's wife abroad, but airports and ports were aware. The Manx ferry crew were scanning passengers, although with no need for a passport on that route, it was a tough job. The Ben-my-Chree had already loaded for the first sailing and there were officers roaming the passenger and car decks. Penny's picture was being shown everywhere. Obviously, the forces further afield were holding a watching brief but as time went on, the chances of them being seen away from Liverpool increased and although there was little to say, there were regular updates to everyone, mainly just to reiterate that she was still missing.

When a call came in on Jordan's mobile, from a number he didn't recognise, he supposed it was another colleague wanting to help. Penny's voice on the line shocked him, taking his breath away, and he reached with his free hand to find a chair as his knees gave way.

"Jordan," she said, "the baby. Have you got the baby? He's in a house in Crosby. Please, please, you have to go and get him!"

Chapter 57

Jordan had to calm his wife. He told her their little boy was safe, that he was with his auntie Lizzie. He waved to attract the attention of the others and told Penny that he was going to put her on speaker.

"Where are you? Penny, are you hurt? Is he still with you?"

Now that she knew her son was okay, Jordan sensed the panic leave her voice. She began to sob.

"No, he's gone," she said. "I don't know where I am. It was just all trees, but I walked back and there was a graveyard and then a church. Jordan, can you come and get me? The vicar let me in. Just a minute."

They heard her speaking to someone.

"I've got it all wrong," she sobbed. "It's not what I said. I don't know what I'm doing." Another murmur in the background and a male voice quietly told them they were in Ince Blundell and gave them directions.

There were many questions and so much to do. They had to stand down the desperate search and reorganise the hunt for Pete, but Jordan had to go to Penny and leave other members of the team to deal with the rest of it.

Stella had already grabbed her coat and was waiting by the door.

It took them ten minutes, speeding down an almost deserted A565. As Stella pulled onto the pavement outside the old graveyard, Jordan was already flinging open the car door and jumping out.

As he crossed the road, the front door of the house opened and a figure in a black tracksuit raised a hand. "Jordan?"

"Yes, are you the vicar?"

The grey-haired man laughed. "Your wife was confused. This hasn't been a church for a while now, though it still has that look about it. But she was so distressed and…" He swept a hand down the front of his body. "I suppose I could give the wrong impression. Anyway, come on in. She's a little calmer now. She's rung her sister and been reassured about the child, Harry, is it?"

"Yes, our son."

There was a noise, and Jordan leaned to look into the hallway. Penny was backlit in a doorway a few metres away. There was a soft plaid blanket around her shoulders. Her hair was dishevelled, a tangled cloud of ebony silk, and as she moved down the narrow space, Jordan saw the glint of tears on her cheeks. Her face was bruised and swollen, and dried blood gathered at the corner of her lips. He reached out and pulled her to him and for just a few minutes they were unaware of anything around them as he rocked her and crooned to her.

Stella and the homeowner stood aside. He smiled at her. She nodded, then gazed around at the pictures on the walls and stared down at the herringbone flooring.

Jordan straightened and although he kept one arm around Penny's shoulders, he reached out a hand for the man to shake and they were ushered into a spacious lounge. There was a whisky bottle on the table and a couple of glasses half empty.

Penny took a deep breath. "I'm an idiot. Mr Evans isn't a vicar. I saw the graveyard and this house with the memorial outside and then he was just there and– well, I assumed…"

"It's fine," the man said. "I'm just glad I was here. I'm often away. That's why we have all the security lights. They woke me. Kids get into the graveyard sometimes, little bleeders, and then into the woods, lighting fires and what not. I'm not sure the lights put them off, but it means the security footage is clear, at least. Anyway, Penny and I were just having a drink. Can I offer anyone anything, or are you on duty?"

"We are, but to be honest, I could use a shot of that." Jordan pointed to the bottle of single malt.

Stella shook her head. "Better not, I'm the driver and I think we still have a fair bit of work to do. I wouldn't turn down a glass of water, though."

The first job was to try to preserve any DNA evidence that might be on Penny's clothing. Stella brought a scene suit from her car and she changed in the cloakroom across the hall from where the others were waiting. Stella took Charles Evan's statement, although he didn't have much to tell them. He hadn't seen the car and the first thing he was aware of were the security lights as Penny staggered into his driveway. There would be footage from his cameras, and he was more than happy to give them copies. He warned them they were trained on his extensive yard, a little on the road and the fences between his property and the woods.

Jordan wanted to take his wife home, but she wouldn't go anywhere until she'd been to the station to make her statement.

"I need to do it while it's still clear in my mind," she said. "Now I know Harry's okay, I can go to Lizzie's afterwards. They were all going to bed anyway. I want to be there when Harry wakes up and I don't want to leave him then. With a bit of luck, he won't remember anything about me leaving him at that horrible house. He was deeply asleep. That bastard let me make sure of that, at least."

They arrived in Copy Lane to a round of applause, though nobody was sure what they were clapping for. Perhaps it was just relief that the boss's family were safe. They still didn't have the murderer and the SIO from the Met would be on his way already. Daylight had brought relief but also an increase in the tension. They all wanted to shine, have the suspect in custody with enough evidence to support a case but that was looking less and less likely.

Chapter 58

Penny was tired. Her face was drawn, and the vicious bruise was swollen and angry-looking. They sat in a family room. It was slightly better than an interview room, but the cheap coffee table was scratched and chipped and the carpet was stained. It smelled stale but was the best they could manage. Kath brought coffee and water and had found some biscuits somewhere, but nobody ate anything. Penny wrapped her hands around the mug that Jordan normally used in the office. There was an image of Harry on the front and her eyes filled with tears as she ran a finger down the picture of his smiling face.

"Are you sure you're up to this, love?" Jordan said.

Penny nodded and reached out to touch his hand. "I want to do it now, while it's still all clear in my mind."

No matter how often they told her it wasn't her fault, she was still insistent that she should have known better. She settled herself on the hard cushions, told them she was ready, and they started the recording.

Pete Roper had turned up at the house and told her that Jordan had sent him.

"I can't believe I let him talk me into getting in the car," Penny said. "But he was so convincing. He said you were hurt, and you'd asked him to come to take me to the hospital." She reached out to clutch at Jordan's hand. "Now, it's so obvious that it was all wrong. I panicked. I always thought I was better than that, but the idea of you injured and me not being there obliterated everything else. There wasn't time to think it through. I just grabbed Harry and left."

Sipping occasionally from the mug and speaking quietly, she told them about the short drive to the dilapidated house. Her voice cracked as she related the awful moment when she realised what was happening. Then the horror when he forced her at knifepoint to give Harry the drugs and wrap up her little boy and leave him sleeping.

"He promised me he'd let you know where he was." She couldn't hold back the tears and for a while there was silence apart from the sounds of her distress. "It was a big knife, like the sort you use in the kitchen. I thought he'd kill us both. He must have been watching us for a while before he got in touch that day. I think he was staying in that house and just planning what to do. It's horrible to think he was out there while we were just going about our lives." She wiped away tears and took a shuddering breath.

Jordan stroked her hand. "Harry's okay. He was fast asleep when we found him. He won't remember anything about it."

Jordan wouldn't tell her yet about the frantic fight to gain access and the fear as he watched Stella carrying the huddled body across the cellar. He might never tell her. She had been through enough, and he believed it was his fault; that he had brought this trouble upon them.

Penny had been desperate; forced to lie on the floor in the back of the car. Pete had ignored her pleas and her tears and threatened her with violence, jabbing the point of his knife into her throat. She touched the red mark with the end of her trembling finger and swallowed. He had struck her more than once and thrown his coat over her.

She had heard him talking to Jordan as he drove but could make no sense of his words.

"I don't know where we went," she said. "I think he was just driving around. Sometimes there was traffic, but mostly just the noise from the car and him muttering to himself or talking on the phone. I tried to listen, to get some useful information, but I'm hopeless. I couldn't do anything except cry."

After what seemed like hours constantly driving, nauseous from her position in the vehicle and from the conviction that she was going to die, Penny heard Pete erupt. "He just lost control completely. He threw the phone out of the window." She had begged him to let her go back and get the baby, but nothing worked. He told her it was too late, and the words had chilled her to the bone. She didn't understand and her desperate pleading aggravated him, but she couldn't stop.

"I'll bet that was when he saw us take down the camera," Stella said.

Penny wiped her eyes. "Whatever it was, he just fell apart. He dragged me out of the back of the car and into the front. We were somewhere dark, with no streetlights. I haven't a clue where it was, by the river, I think. I tried to get away. That was when he hit me again." She touched the swollen skin under her eye and lifted her sleeve to let them see the angry red mark on her wrist.

Jordan pulled her closer to him. Of all the things that Pete had done, laying hands on Penny angered him the most. He felt his own urge to kill and fought it down.

"If it was when we took down the camera. Harry was already safe by then," Jordan said.

"He must have seen John climbing up that bloody ladder, though," Stella said. "So, he knew we were on to him and must have guessed we were going to read the SD card. He knew by that time that we'd seen the car, and we were coming for him, the evil bastard. He probably thought we didn't know how the bloody things work. Well, to be honest, I didn't, not until now."

Penny shook her head. She didn't know what had made him fall apart; at what point in the night he had lost control. It had been sudden and extreme. "I think it had all just got completely out of hand and he was lost. He tried to tell me about his partner and wanted me to believe that he hadn't meant to kill him. He said he'd got the gun just to scare him, and it was all a terrible mistake. The gun was supposed to be given back, unused. He couldn't do that once he'd fired it, so he'd lost a pile of money. Now he reckons the bloke he rented it from might be after him. He's terrified they'll find him, and they won't let him live because he can identify them. He kept saying he didn't mean to do it and he was sorry. I think he wanted me to feel sympathy for him. Antony was leaving him." She shrugged. "He said he'd lost everything and didn't know where to turn and then he thought of you, his mate doing well in the police, who could help. That's what he said, anyway. They had the property up here so that's why he ended up in Crosby. He doesn't know you, Jordan. If he knew you, he would never have come. He thought you could make it all go away." She paused and drank a final mouthful of the cold coffee.

"I tried to convince him that the best thing was to give himself up," she continued. "We were still driving, but he didn't know where we were, where we were going, and what he was going to do with me. By then, I don't think he wanted to kill me. I thought he would have done it if he was going to and he'd left it too late and he must have realised he'd completely cocked up and couldn't get away. So, he just had to get rid of me and I sat in that car and waited." She gulped and shook her head. "That's what I told myself, anyway."

She was calm now, and her account was factual and clear. She was speaking so quietly that Jordan leaned closer to listen.

"He said he loved his partner. That's not true. You don't shoot someone you love."

She lay her head against the grubby sofa back and closed her eyes. "I don't know where he's gone. He stopped the car and pushed me out and drove off. As he left me, he told me to tell you he was sorry, Jordan. I think he's crazy. I'm worried about what will happen to him now." It was testament to her kindness that, after everything, she still had compassion to spare.

"We're watching out for him. He won't get far," Jordan said.

John cracked open the door and raised a questioning eyebrow at Jordan.

Penny told him to go. "I'm fine. If you can get someone to take me to Lizzie's, I'll see you there later. You just go and find him."

* * *

John was running the CCTV footage on his computer. "We see the bottom of the car as it passes the house. He's out of range when he stops to get your missus out, but the lights are reflected on the graveyard wall. Then we see her come back and walk up the path."

"Okay, so then he heads into the woods, yes? Have we got people out there looking for him?" Jordan said.

John shook his head and frowned. "We haven't got the bods. There's been a bit of a bust-up at one of the clubs in town and a running battle through the centre. Everyone was diverted once they knew we had your wife safe."

"Shit. I don't suppose there'll be coverage out beyond the village, will there?"

"There isn't, boss. But..." John stopped. "This could well be nothing. But if you watch..." He pointed at the screen. "Do you see? There's your Penny. Sorry, that must be rotten for you to have to watch. But... behind her."

"What? I don't know what you mean," Jordan said.

"I reckon he's come back. That time of night, that little place, what are the chances of two cars? I know sod's law and all that, but I reckon it's him. On the way back to town. There's a turning up the road and he could have done a uey and been on his way back to the city when we got Penny's call."

"Right. Footage of anything we can get in Ince. I'm going to take Penny to her sister's and then I'm coming back."

"One of the women could take her."

The look Jordan gave him precluded any further suggestion that he might hand his wife over to anyone else.

"I'll be back, quick as I can. In the meantime, get Kath and Vi on the live footage, traffic cameras, and anything else."

Chapter 59

The team was running on adrenalin and coffee, but no one had gone home. John raised his head as Jordan came into the room. "Sorry boss, nothing yet – no traffic cameras and no buses running so early. We can knock on doors later, when people are getting up. There might be some doorbell cameras."

They all knew it would be pointless after so much time had passed. For now, the Jaguar had vanished into the darkness. Most of them were focusing on the idea that Pete had headed back to the city, except Kath, who thought it was more realistic to watch the motorways. She'd been right often in the past. But it was less than twenty minutes from where they had seen the lights, which they were convinced was Pete's car, to Switch Island and then he would be well away on the routes out of the city.

They all believed they had missed him, and the search would soon be nationwide. It was disheartening, but no one could bring themselves to call a halt.

Jordan stood in front of the corkboard. There were images of the car, the gun, and a picture of Pete that had been forwarded from London. Later, they would send a SOCO team to examine the house in Crosby where his wife and little boy had been held captive, abused and drugged. His fists clenched as he looked at the pictures John had taken of the room where Pete had lived while he watched them and made his plans. Fury boiled in his gut. In a few hours, a senior officer would arrive and effectively take over and they would no doubt make much of the fact that Pete had been there, and they had lost him. Although it would be done according to protocol and with all the right words said, it would be taken out of the hands of Copy Lane.

Just having him found wasn't enough. Jordan wanted to be the one to find him. He wanted to fasten the cuffs on his wrists and read him his rights and look him in the eye as he let him know that not everyone was driven by greed and weakness. Even as he acknowledged that addiction was an illness, he couldn't forgive the harm that had been done to his family.

He reached for his coat. "Stel, I'm just going out for a bit. Back soon. If DI Keogh arrives, can you deal with him?"

"Of course I can, boss. But don't you want me to come with you? Are you okay?"

"Yes, just something I have to do."

She shrugged her shoulders, puzzled, and perhaps a little offended, he thought, but so be it.

The world was awake now and the roads beginning to hum with traffic. Not the full-blown rush hour, but enough to slow his progress. Jordan called Penny on the hands-free, and she told him she was fine.

"I tried to get some kip, but I just can't settle. I want to be in the house with you and Harry," she said. "I keep thinking about the mess in the kitchen and I want it cleared up. I want to scrub the whole episode away and reclaim our space."

"We will soon. I just have a couple of things I want to do and then I'll come and take you home."

By the time he arrived, the streets were busy with schoolchildren, joggers, and commuters. It was all very normal, too normal for what he had in his mind. This was most likely a mistake, but there was nothing else he could do, and it was better than waiting around and watching the team searching for something nobody believed they would find.

The makeshift gate was pushed aside, and Jordan couldn't remember how they had left it. He parked illegally with two wheels on the pavement and was rewarded with a glare from a woman wheeling a buggy. There was no sign of the Jaguar, but he had to make absolutely sure the place was deserted. He strode across the messy front yard and glanced at the skip rusting in the corner. The rotten old ladder lay against the front wall and cables from the camera dangled from the soffit boards. The lock was gone from the front door guard.

He remembered the pile of builder's sand at the end of the side passage and chose the other route to access the back garden. As he turned the corner, scraps of roof tile and debris fell onto the paving and he looked up towards the apex roof. There was nothing to see from the acute angle of his vision and he stepped backwards onto the wet grass. High on the roof, a small dormer window had been opened, the metal shield had slid across the slope and was caught on the guttering. As he peered up, another cascade of rubbish rained down and from behind the four-pot chimney, he saw a pair of feet pushing against the slope and trousered legs braced on the wet tiles. He watched as Pete slid on his backside, holding onto the chimney with one arm and clasping a knife in his other hand, which he was also using to steady himself as he moved forward nearer and nearer to the edge of the roof.

Chapter 60

Jordan didn't think he had been seen and for the moment, that was the best advantage he could have. He moved back towards the house and along to where the cellar window was still open to the elements. Dropping down into the well, he paused for a moment to send a message to John and Stella.

At the house. Pete here. Going in. Alert Fire Services.

He noted that there was no reception, but once he climbed out of the basement room, the phone would find a signal and the message would be sent.

Broken glass crunched under his feet and his shirt caught on one of the rusty bars John had removed. It was a squeeze. John had thought he wouldn't be able to but he wriggled through. There was no other option.

Inside, he turned on his phone torch and stepped as lightly as he could on the edges of the damp and crumbling wood of the cellar staircase. The door at the top was open, and he walked along the hallway.

He paused at the bottom of the stairs and listened. From here there was nothing but the cooing of a pigeon somewhere in the roof of the old building and the creak of timber as the day outside warmed.

The first floor was dark, cold, and bleak. There was a filthy carpet on the floor and though it was unpleasantly mouldy and stank of wet, rotting wool, it deadened his footsteps as he went towards the next flight of stairs, listening now for anything that might indicate Pete had come back from the roof and into the house.

The flight of steps to the attic floor was steep, and the banister was coming away from the wall. It rattled when he gripped it, so he used his hand on the spalling plaster to steady himself. In the room, cold air blew in through the open window and leaves and debris shushed and rattled across the floor.

From his position at the side of the dormer, he couldn't see the chimney, but he could hear movement on the roof. Pete was muttering to himself. The words were indistinct, but the occasional sob and a strange hissing sound were clear. The man was obviously distressed. If Jordan appeared suddenly on the tiles, the result could be catastrophic. Equally, shouting through the open window would be next to pointless.

He pulled out his phone. At this height, there was a good signal. His message had gone, and he knew colleagues would already be on the way. All he had to do was keep things calm until help arrived.

It was possible Pete still had the phone he had been using to communicate, and Jordan clicked on the contact icon.

> *Mate, things have got out of hand. Give us the chance to talk it through. Penny and Harry are okay, so you don't have to worry about all that. A bloke is coming from London, but I'll talk to him for you. We can sort things out.*

He pressed send and waited. He heard a chime. There was a small shuffle as more debris fell from the roof. The muttering resumed.

The response came quickly. Just two words, universally clear in meaning, and he heard the clatter as Pete flung the phone from the roof and it smashed on the patio far below.

Jordan puffed out his cheeks. He leaned into the open window space and called out that he was there; that he only wanted to help, and he was coming out.

Chapter 61

Jordan clambered onto the window ledge and leaned out to look at the pitched roof of wet slates, moss, and bird guano. Eyes closed for a moment, he took a deep breath to steady his nerves. He wrapped his fingers around the frame of the dormer and hauled himself up and out. Debris and moss slid from under his feet to join the other muck in the back garden below. He slithered crabwise on his behind along the roof. He swivelled and slid, pushing and levering with feet and hands until he was at the corner and could see the chimney where Pete sat. His arms were around the brick structure, the knife lay across his legs which were stretched down the slope towards the guttering.

"Mate, can you just come in? Really, this isn't doing my heart rate any good," Jordan said. "Let's just get inside and go from there, only I am not a happy bunny up here."

The other man turned a grubby, tear-stained face to look at Jordan and shook his head.

"Go in, Crackers. It's over. I'm sorry about Penny and your lad."

Jordan had never done the negotiator course, but it was clear that he had to keep things calm and the conversation going until help arrived.

"They're okay. She was a bit shook up, of course she was, but it's all fine now."

"I'm glad, and Harry?"

"Yes, back home, so there's nothing to worry about."

"Ha, don't give me that. You know. You have to know what's happened. Don't even pretend you don't."

There was no point lying so Jordan admitted he had been told the worst of it. "You'll have to answer for what you did, Pete. There's no way around that, but you're a young man. You can serve your time and then try to make a new life. Come on. I know you must be in pain. You must be grieving for Antony. It's time to mend things." Then he realised it had been a mistake.

At the naming of his boyfriend, Pete let out a sob and shook his head violently from side to side. He slid a little on the slick tiles and grabbed out to hold more tightly onto the chimney. Maybe he wasn't intending to throw himself over after all. If that was the case, though, why was he up here?

"Pete, what are you doing, mate? Why don't you just come on in? It'll play better if you give yourself up."

Pete leaned forward. He picked up a small piece of broken slate and threw it over the edge of the roof.

"Nah. I reckon I might as well call it quits. Nothing left for me." He lifted the knife and turned it back and forth. It glinted in the early sunlight. He raised it to his throat.

Jordan's heart jumped. Bile flooded up from his stomach. "Don't!" As he called out, he turned onto his knees. "Don't be stupid, Pete." He moved forward on all fours across the slope of the roof.

Pete watched. He lowered the knife again and laughed, one short sharp sound.

"What do you look like? You know, I always thought you were cool. All the girls were after you. Even though none of us had any money, you always looked good. Sharp. Clean. What do you look like now? You're filthy. You look scared to death. I've never seen you look so bloody ridiculous."

"Yeah, okay," Jordan said. "I'm scared. If you must know, I'm bloody terrified. This is my idea of torment. No, no, it's no good." As he spoke, he turned back to a sitting position. He raised a hand to swipe across his forehead. "I can't do it. Shit, I can't move. How the hell am I going to get back in?"

"Just do it, go on. Leave me."

Jordan moved his feet, and another shutter of detritus scattered over the guttering. He made a noise, a cross between a groan and a gasp.

"Stop buggering about, just go back inside. This'll be over in a minute," Pete said. "Look, your friends have arrived." He leaned forward and Jordan reached out a hand.

"Don't, don't do that. Keep still, you nutter. You'll be over the edge if you're not careful."

Pete turned to look. "You really are scared, aren't you?" he said.

"Bloody terrified. I can't move," Jordan gasped. "Help me, Pete, just help me get back to the window, and I'll let you do whatever you want. I'll try to get you out of this if I can. There's stuff I can do." Jordan lowered his head. He was panting rapidly, his shoulders shaking.

"Oh, for pity's sake. I never would have believed this. The great Jordan Carr, a whimpering wuss." As he spoke, Pete tucked the knife into the waistband of his trousers. He used his hands on the side of the chimney to pull himself to a crouching position and walked on his knees to where Jordan sat with his eyes closed, his fingers digging into a gap between the slates. As Pete approached, Jordan looked up and reached out to him.

Now he was within arm's reach. Jordan twisted and, in a graceful unfurling movement, he pushed up from his seat on the wet roof, stood with his knees slightly bent for balance, and took the cuffs from the holder on his belt. He took two steady steps across the space, bent and grabbed the other man around the shoulders. He snatched the knife from the belt, called out a warning to Stella, and tossed it back towards the chimney where it slid downwards. Grabbing Pete by the arms, he dragged him backwards until he was stretched across the slope. He rolled him over and pulled his arms behind him, snapping on the cuffs, whilst placing a knee in the middle of his back. Now he stood straight and tall, his feet planted firmly on the roof. He looked over the edge and waved to Stella, who was peering up from the path at the side of the house.

"You bastard," Pete gasped.

"Yeah, that's me." Jordan couldn't keep the amusement from his voice. "There was a reason I was Hamlet, and you were only the gravedigger. I always was a better actor. Peter Roper, I am arresting you on suspicion of the abduction, imprisonment, and actual bodily harm of Penelope Carr, also the child abduction of Harry Carr." He finished reciting the rights, turned and walked steadily across the roof, dragging Pete on his knees behind him. The murder charge and the financial issues could be dealt with by DI Keogh. It might go some way to make up for the undeniable errors Jordan had made. It didn't matter. He had the person who had laid hands on his wife and child. For now, it was enough.

Chapter 62

"Honest to God, boss, I was having kittens when I saw you on that roof. I was sure you were going to fall," Stella said.

"One of my cousins is a roofer," Jordan said. "I used to help him in the school holidays. It's just a question of confidence. Yes, it was a bit unstable, but I was never that worried."

"Never?" she said.

"Nope, oh well, okay a bit, but more that the tiles would break, and we'd go through."

They turned to watch as the fire tender drove away and Pete was tucked into prisoner transport for the trip to Copy Lane.

"I'll go back and get him settled in the custody suite. I'm having a break then, and does anyone fancy a brew round my place before we go back in later?" Jordan asked.

"Always," John said. "What about Penny?"

"I'll go for her later. She sent a message to say she wants to spend some time with her sister. She doesn't want to be in the house on her own. I'll let her know when I'm back. Everything okay, Stel?"

"Yeah. I'm fine. Well, I will be in a bit when my heart gets back to normal." She laughed and then held up the phone she had been looking at to show them a message. "Kath says DCI Lewis is going to look after the DI from London. He's thrilled that we've caught Roper. Can't wait to let Keogh know and tell him we're fine with him having the collar for the murder and what have you. I know that was a foregone conclusion, but it would have been nice to let you have some input, boss."

"No surprise there then," Jordan said. "It doesn't matter. It's what I was hoping for anyway. Should ease any ill feeling. You're not bothered about that, are you?"

"No, it's not that. I was scanning the overnight reports. Fazakerley North have arrested Jean Court's son."

"What for?" he asked.

"Benno. Beat him up at the scrapyard last night. Used an iron bar, apparently. He's in Fazakerley Hospital. His condition is extremely serious."

"Shit. We should have seen it coming."

"Well, I guess we did in a way, but there was nothing more we could do, boss. He'd been warned off. We couldn't baby sit Benno, and Steve Court hadn't broken any laws up to that point."

"What about the other lad, Stick?"

"No. Nothing about him. I think he's still poorly so at home with his mam. Doesn't seem that he was at the scrapyard anyway."

"I'll go round the hospital this affie if you like," John said. "Give you time with your wife and your little lad."

"Thanks. Let me know how he is. I'll liaise with Fazakerley North and see if I can sit in on the interviews. We warned him, why didn't he listen?"

No one had an answer. Jordan glanced down at this filthy clothes and dirty hands. He could nip home and change, but it seemed like too much trouble and there was a tracksuit in his locker at work.

They pulled the temporary gate back into place and Stella brought scene-of-crime tape from her car to secure the entrance. There was a resigned-looking uniformed officer trying not to seem too put upon standing guard until a SOCO team could be found to attend. All in good time, they would need what evidence they could gather to present to the CPS, but right now they wanted to sit behind their desks and start to put the whole thing away.

Chapter 63

The inspector at Fazakerley North had no problem with letting Jordan sit in while they spoke to Steve Court. Jean's son had requested a solicitor, and they were waiting for a legal aid lawyer to be brought in. They sat in the office, going over the information from the post office raid and what came after.

Steve had been caught by Benno's uncle as he ran away from the scrapyard. Although he didn't realise who he was and what he had been up to, the older man had given chase in his van when he spotted the iron bar. He cornered Steve in the access to one of the other units and when he saw the blood on his clothes and the fear in his face, he had called the emergency services and kept him cornered with the old white van.

Apparently, he had given up without a fight and said he had no regrets and just wished he'd killed the other lad, which was going to make it a tricky job for the lawyer when he eventually arrived. All Steve could hope for was sympathy for the death of his mother, which might go some way to reducing his sentence.

It was midway through the afternoon before the interview was underway, but it was short, with Steve Court remanded in custody because there was still a risk to Stick if he was allowed to go home.

Milly Court had sat in the reception area, alternating between sobbing into tissues and swearing at the passing officers, berating them for 'letting crims walk free and picking on people who were only sticking up for themselves'.

Jordan was tempted to leave by another door, but his conscience took him out to speak to the young woman. "I'm really sorry, Milly. We warned Steve not to do this. I understand that he wanted to do something but taking the law into your own hands never ends well."

"You understand," she spat at him. "How the hell can you understand? I bet your family has never had to go through something like this."

He had no response that wouldn't sound as if he were trying to match trauma for trauma and so he told her again how sorry he was and left for home. Someone had been tasked with warning Stick's family to be aware, but with Steve locked up, the risk was surely minimal. He didn't imagine Milly would try to avenge her mum, but you never knew.

John rang from the hospital with the news that Benno was out of immediate danger, but the chances were he would lose the sight in one eye. It was sad and sordid and depressing.

Jordan had had enough of it all and so he drove home with Bruce Springsteen as loud as he could bear it on his sound system to drown out the regret and guilt swirling in his brain.

John and Stella arrived soon after. It wasn't the celebration it might have been. They were all subdued and tired and Jordan decided they needed Irish coffees and chocolate. That brought a smile to John's face, at least.

They were drinking a second cup of coffee and eating warm brownies when they heard a car in the drive.

Penny fell into Jordan's arms as he opened the door. Lizzie was holding Harry, who was desperate to get down and tell his dad and Aunty Stella how he had 'fall'd asleep at the man's house and then woken up at Aunty Lizzie's'.

"He doesn't remember anything about the hospital," Penny said. "It's good, but also a bit scary."

After Stella and John left, Jordan sat with his wife and son in the living room, quiet and thankful.

"I'm going in for a while later," he told Penny. "Will you be okay?"

She reassured him she'd be fine and determined not to let what had happened make her unhappy in their home.

"I'm going to clean the place, top to bottom. I'm going to get rid of any trace of that man," she said.

"I'm sorry, love. I should never have brought him here."

"Don't be silly. None of it is your fault, and it's done and over with. Will you go for a drink after? You know, the successful collar celebration?"

He said he wasn't sure what was going to happen because the team weren't in until the next day, and even then, he didn't know that they'd be up for it.

"Okay, well, it's a shame to waste a good clean of the house, so why don't you bring Stella and John back and I'll make something nice? We'll have a couple of drinks here."

He nodded, and she wrapped her arms around his waist and looked up into his face. "What's the matter? Is it because he was your friend? He deserves what he has coming to him. You know that, don't you?"

"No, it's not that at all. It's the reverse. Okay, he'll be going to jail for the murder. What he did to you and Harry will be secondary in real terms and so probably the sentence for that will be served concurrently. It'll be on his record for what it's worth, but it doesn't feel like enough. Then there's the rest of it he'll never pay for at all. All the lives that have been ruined and especially poor Jean Court. She wanted some cigarettes and a pizza, and she was just there by chance. If Benno hadn't found the gun and Daz hadn't been so unhappy at home, all of that, then Jean Court would probably still be alive. Ultimately, though, it all comes back to him, to Pete, and he won't even give them a thought."

Penny knew there was nothing she could say to make him feel better. Life is unfair and inexplicable things happen. She held him a little tighter and lay her head on his chest. They listened to the birds in the garden and Harry playing with his cars in the living room. He'd put this behind him, she knew that. She'd try to do the same because they had to go on. They couldn't let the bad guys win.

The End

List of characters

Detective Inspector Jordan Carr – Jamaican heritage. Married with one little boy, Harry. Lives in Crosby. Drives a VW Golf.

Penny – Jordan's wife. Works for the Citizens Advice Bureau.

Lizzie – Penny's sister.

Detective Sergeant Stella May – Liverpool, born and bred. Lives in Aintree.

Nana Gloria – Jordan's grandmother. Lives in London with his extended family.

Detective Constable John Grice – Regular part of Jordan's team. A Scouser who lives in Old Skelmersdale with his father.

DCI Josh Lewis – Detective Chief Inspector in charge at Copy Lane.

Detective Constable Kath Webster – Junior officer who has recently had a knee replacement.

Detective Constable Violet Purcell – Junior officer. Has spent all her working life in the force and is retiring in five years.

Karen – DCI Lewis's secretary.

Ted Bliss – Crime scene sergeant. Sarcastic and funny but also sympathetic.

Dr James Jasper – Medical examiner based at the University of Liverpool and Liverpool Central Morgue.

Pete Roper – Jordan's friend from his schooldays.

Amy Finch – Shop cleaner.

Lilian Goudy – Shop manager.

Julia Bull – Staff at the shop and witness.

Jean Court – Victim.

Milly Court – Jean's daughter.

Steve Court – Jean's son.

Stick – Simon Brown – Scouse teenager.

Daz – Daniel Burdon – Scouse teenager.

Benno – Benjamin Midgely – Scouse teenager.

Brian Marsden – Head teacher.

Detective Inspector Paul Keogh – Met Police. SIO on the murder in London.

PC Sharon Taylor – Young Liverpudlian uniformed officer.

If you enjoyed this book, please let others know by leaving a quick review on Amazon. Also, if you spot anything untoward in the paperback, get in touch. We strive for the best quality and appreciate reader feedback.

editor@thebookfolks.com

www.thebookfolks.com

Other titles of interest

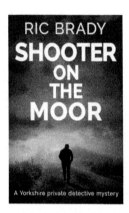

SHOOTER ON THE MOOR by Ric Brady

A sleepy Yorkshire village has a rude awakening when a jogger is shot dead on the surrounding moorland. Local retired cop Henry Ward heads to the scene and meets some of his former colleagues, who agree to him doing some detective work on the side. Ward is soon on the trail of the murder gun, but is he ready to face down the person holding it?

CATFISH by Sadie Norman

It is not without some malice that rookie detective Anna
McArthur is called "crazy" by her colleagues. She certainly
tends to act first and think later. But when Anna discovers
the body of a murdered woman who has "catfish" carved
into her chest, she feels a personal duty to do everything
she can to up her game and find the killer.

Sign up to our mailing list to find out about new releases and special offers!

www.thebookfolks.com

Printed in Great Britain
by Amazon

47200132R00121